Praise for the works of B

Hero(ine) Addict

This is actually a very pleasant romantic tale with serious undertones, specifically families living through issues of mental illness and childhood cancer. The author did an excellent job of weaving these very significant issues into an adorable romance between Eliot and Harper.

The writing in this story is excellent. The illnesses are handled in a very compassionate manner, and the characters are realistic. I am glad that I read this book. It is a beautiful story, and I enjoyed reading it. I will also be looking for more from this author.

-Betty H., *NetGalley*

Bait and Switch

Besides the great characters, I really enjoyed the romance. It went at the perfect pace. No insta-love here. In fact, this book stays away from many common tropes found in lesfic romance. I don't want to say what they are, cause it would be too much of a spoiler, but I will say I was impressed and happy. This is one of those really feel good romances. I'm happy right now, and I enjoy that feeling. While this book deals with a few tough subjects, it does it with a dose of humor and wonderful dialog, which just helps to make a great reading experience.

-Lext Kent's Reviews, *goodreads*

Sleeping Dogs Lie

Cochrane has given us an endearing, though somewhat self-deprecating sleuth in Maddie Smithwick. She's also given us a comical and often annoying sidekick in the form of best friend Dottie. In spite of herself, Dottie is an endearing character, especially because she's loyal to Maddie. These two are definitely a mismatched pair, yet their relationship works. *Sleeping Dogs Lie* is an entertaining read. Parenthetical remarks throughout the story make us feel as if we are privy to little secrets about Maddie, her friends, and the subject of her probing. This offering by E.J. Cochrane is a good first effort. If this story is the introduction of a series with the loveable yet insecure Matilda Smithwick, it promises to be a delightful one.

-Lambda Literary Review

Hounded

Oh my goodness where to start. The language has a strong cozy mystery vibe, with unerringly witty dialogue, a fast paced, twisty plot, and a great setting. Every classic trope of a cozy is on display in this book, but with small tweaks that give the book a fresh feel.

-The Lesbian Review

…*Hounded* is a captivating and fast-paced novel that will keep readers hooked until the very end. E.J. Cochrane's storytelling prowess shines through, offering a thrilling blend of mystery and supernatural elements. With its well-drawn characters, atmospheric settings, and unpredictable twists, this book is a must-read for fans of the genre.

-Sylvia G., *NetGalley*

Christmissed

Other Bella Books by Blythe H. Warren

My Best Friend's Girl
Bait and Switch
Hero(ine) Addict

About the Author

Blythe H. Warren survived fifteen years as a college English teacher before calling it quits. Now she has a much less stressful career in retail. Her first novel was a Lammy finalist, she won a Goldie for her second novel, *Bait and Switch*, and she writes the Matilda Smithwick mysteries under her real name (E.J. Cochrane). When she's not working or writing, she's training for her next marathon (which she always swears will be her last one). She and her partner live with their ball-obsessed pit bull, Gonzo, and his adoring feline fan club: Beatrix, Juniper, Aoife and Henry.

Christmissed

Blythe H. Warren

BELLA
BOOKS

Bella Books, Inc.
P.O. Box 10543
Tallahassee, FL 32302

First Edition - 2024

Editor: Heather Flournoy

ISBN: 978-1-64247-603-3

Acknowledgments

I never would have finished writing this book if not for the tough love and unflagging support of an amazing group of women—Jennie Tyderek, Diane Piña and Lynda Fitzgerald, I am so fortunate to know all of you. I can't thank you enough for all of the emails, texts, virtual and in-person conversations. You helped me find my way when I didn't think I'd ever reach the end. Heidi would be proud. Thanks also to my friend Amanda Sears for sharing tales of her time working with a food stylist and to my friend Sharon Reinheimer for a last-minute, lightning-fast beta read—I promise I'll give you more time on the next one. My editor, Heather Flournoy, worked with me through my ridiculous schedule and every obstacle I threw in our shared path, and she absolutely made this a better book. I'm truly grateful for her insights as well as her time and patience (not to mention her appreciation for my love of asides). To everyone at Bella, thank you for all you do. I could not be more proud to put my work in your hands. Finally, to my partner, Sue Hawks, you are my favorite person to brainstorm with. I'm ready to dream up new ideas whenever you are.

Dedication

For the Mary Anns, and for all of us who've learned
the value of found family.

PART ONE

Winter

CHAPTER ONE

"Bah humbug," Winter grumbled and immediately felt guilty. It wasn't Christmas's fault that she was miserable.

No, that blame belonged solely to the woman whose existence had upended Winter's entire life. Here it was, the first day of December—a day normally reserved for revelry in the form of tree trimming, light stringing, and general holiday décor merriment—but rather than adorning her home with all the glorious trappings of the season, she was lingering in bed, hiding from the world and contemplating life as a hermit.

"And now she's ruined Christmas for me, too," she muttered, her voice muffled by the pillow she'd pulled over her face in the middle of the night, as if she could hide from her thoughts. She'd been desperate to silence her entirely unhelpful internal monologue but, failing that, had half hoped to suffocate herself enough to nod off. It hadn't quieted her restless mind any, but it had proved an enticing spot for her kitten to doze.

Had they progressed further in their bonding by this point, Winter might have dislodged the slumbering kitten. This early in their relationship, however, she felt she still needed to prove herself to Cloris, and ejecting her from atop her plush personal mattress would do little to advance Winter's cause. Sighing, she stretched her arms and legs, careful not to jostle Cloris's pedestal.

She refused to open her eyes and face the world, not that she would see much beyond the festive turkeys strutting across her flannel pillowcase. She had so much work to do and no drive to do it. She was already behind by almost a week, and clearly, hiding under her covers wouldn't help her accomplish anything. Resigned to making something of her day, she gingerly groped the top of her pillow, cringing when her hand touched something moist.

"Dear god, I hope that was your nose." A querulous meow was the kitten's only reply. "That wasn't very reassuring," Winter groaned, and wiped her hand on the pillowcase. She had to wash the bedding anyway now that it was time to ditch the turkeys for Santa and snowmen. Or maybe prancing reindeer would put her more in the holiday mood.

Either way, she had to get herself out of bed without disturbing the now purring tiny ball of black fluff whose mercurial sweetness, coupled with a somewhat unconventional interpretation of cuddling, put her already flagging motivation at a severe disadvantage. If she forcibly removed Cloris, the young cat might rebuff Winter, who balked at a repeat of the cold shoulder she'd received following the Tampon Incident of early November. The ostracism seemed especially unfair given that Winter hadn't exactly enjoyed prying a bloody wad of cotton from Cloris's razor-sharp claws, nor had she relished the subsequent babyproofing of her bathroom garbage can while her kitten threw shade at her.

That Cloris was now sleeping with Winter, in an undoubtedly adorable, albeit unorthodox, fashion, showed real progress in their relationship, progress she didn't want to jeopardize. But she couldn't lie here all day, no matter how enticing the thought. If she could somehow climb out of bed while preserving Cloris's cozy perch, she stood a real chance of maintaining their current level of affection with the added bonus of feeling like she'd accomplished something that day.

"Challenge accepted," she said and began scooting herself lower in the bed.

Once she'd inched far enough from the headboard, she delicately slid the pillow off her head, holding her breath until she was certain that both pillow and kitten were safely settled on the bed. Unfortunately, by then her pajama bottoms had burrowed deep into crevices better left vacant, and she had also managed to truss her legs in the chaos of her sheets.

As she tugged and kicked simultaneously, hoping to extract her feet from their flannel prison, she reconsidered the merits of tucking her sheets in—it wasn't as if anyone would be seeing her bed anytime soon, and clearly it was a hazard. On the plus side, after this workout, she could skip the gym today. With one final thrust, she liberated her entire body from both the bedding and the bed and landed on the floor with a thud, bruised but triumphant.

Before she could savor her victory, however, Cloris rose, flaunted her lithe agility with a near-acrobatic stretch, and hopped to the floor at Winter's feet, essentially rendering her protracted battle with her bedding moot. The kitten meowed and pawed Winter's leg before strutting out of the room, undoubtedly on a path toward the kitchen. She paused at the door to toss another plaintive cry over her shoulder. Winter had no choice but to follow.

Most people, Winter assumed, would simply empty the contents of a can of cat food on a plate and consider that a job well done. But presentation was everything, and a can-shaped blob of brown pâté on a plate hardly qualified as appetizing. True, Cloris had yet to notice the array of feline-themed plates chosen specifically for her dining experience, nor did she appreciate any of the garnishes that Winter had adorned her meals with, but not for lack of trying. And at least the kitten had played with the parsley before drowning it in her water.

"Where should we start?" she asked, one eye on the painfully sluggish drip of her coffee maker.

In any other year, just the anticipation of the impending holiday season would be more than enough to perk her up and fuel her day—she might savor a cup of hot cocoa as she began the days-long process of transforming her home into a holiday haven that Santa himself would envy, but it was more festive treat than required jolt. Cloris briefly glanced up from her mackerel and sardines in lobster consommé and blinked. "You're right. Just dive in."

She told Alexa to play holiday music throughout the house—and only had to correct her twice—then made her way to the Christmas closet. She considered that it was perhaps excessive to devote an entire walk-in closet to one holiday. On the other hand, if she continued accumulating Christmas keepsakes and curios, she might have to invest in an addition to house her collection. The sound of sleigh bells brought an unconscious smile to her face, a smile that dimmed noticeably as the voice of pop superstar Meadow Lane filled her ears with Christmas cheer and painful reminders.

Cloris wound around her legs then tapped the closet door, reminding Winter to focus on the present. Ready to get this over with, she grabbed the first bin she saw and, after removing Cloris from the garland in which she'd managed to swathe herself, she placed the box on her dining room table, establishing it as Christmas Central. Once she'd divested the box of its jolly assemblage of elves and reindeer, trees and bells, holly and wreaths, it became the winter residence of her everyday décor. She cleaned her home as she went, telling Cloris about each piece as she carefully positioned it on the shelf it occupied every December.

Halfway through the first carton of Christmas curios, her breath caught when she picked up the origami reindeer from Avery. True, it looked more like a misshapen owl than any kind of festive ruminant, but she'd loved it so much when Avery gave it to her, she looked past its unique appearance. She'd forgotten it was hiding on her bookshelf, and seeing it again brought back a flood of memories that she had no desire to revisit. Without comment, she dropped it in the box and closed the lid, earning a reproachful meow from Cloris.

"I don't need attitude from you right now, missy."

But the kitten had already embarked upon a round of fervent ablutions, her concern over Winter's heartache apparently a thing of the past. Thankfully, the ping of an incoming text saved her from a one-sided argument with her kitten.

It's a good day to hang lights. You supply the ladder. I'll bring the nog?

Gabe had been her self-appointed helper elf for the past six years. It wouldn't be Christmas without his peevish assistance.

I think I'm going to skip Christmas this year, she answered, though she didn't completely feel that way.

Blasphemer! he replied. *You just need some extra holiday cheer to get you out of your funk. We'll swing by this afternoon.*

Fair warning—I'm not very jolly.

That's different how? You haven't been jolly since Avery left.

"Maybe that's because she broke my heart and ruined my favorite time of year," she said and pocketed her phone. She scooped up her box of everyday decorations and headed back to the Christmas closet, resigned to make some holiday headway before Gabe and Noah showed up. In spite of herself, she pulled the paper reindeer out of the box again. "It is still kind of cute." She sighed as she set it on her nightstand, a semi welcome token of a trying year.

"If only I hadn't run into her."

CHAPTER TWO

The previous February

Winter didn't really believe in hell, but as she glued yet another sesame seed on yet another hamburger bun, she began to suspect she was being punished for something. It wasn't as if she'd never before devoted hours to a tedious task in order to please a client. Nor did she object to putting her attention to detail to good use, at least not generally speaking. But this was day five of ridiculous requests coupled with robust indecision, a losing combination that had done nothing but waste everyone's time. All week, she'd outdone herself to meet the curious demands of her client only to be told at the last minute that he wasn't sure that was the right direction—never mind that this was his cookbook, and as such, every recipe and, therefore, every direction was his. As the week had progressed, so had the client's maddening blend of indecisive particularity. She'd gone from presenting him with a dizzying array of salads—green, fruit, pasta, creamy, and otherwise—none of which were exactly what he had in mind, despite all of them coming directly from his cookbook—to the freezer fiasco, to this. A perfectly seeded burger bun battalion ready to be rejected as soon as her client appeared on the scene.

When she'd first been approached about styling for a summer cookbook, her mind had filled with all the interesting possibilities and challenges of such a task—from making potato salad appear more appealing than a blob of mayonnaise, boiled eggs, and potatoes had any right to look, to capturing a perfectly melting pat of butter on gorgeously steaming corn on the cob, to all the inherent difficulties of pitting ice cream against harsh studio lights. Even after courting hypothermia in the walk-in freezer just to get the perfect shot, she'd happily repeat that experience if it meant she never had to see another sesame seed.

By the time this finished project was in people's hands, she'd be up to her elbows in turkey, cranberries, and pumpkins, in anticipation of the holiday season. It was a somewhat off-kilter way to live—one foot in the current world, the other leaping toward the next season and any feasts associated with it. But she found it oddly comforting to be surrounded by the trappings of the holiday season in the midst of a sweltering summer. Left to her own devices, she'd have year-round Christmas. The world would be covered in snow, and everyone would walk around in their ugly holiday sweaters or swaddled in cozy fleece, smiling and cheerful, ready to celebrate. There'd be scarves and hot cocoa, not to mention snowballs and ice skating. The world would be magical all year long. But instead of magic, she had sesame seeds, glue fumes and six hours to go. Hopefully.

The crime, she supposed, was ever agreeing to work for Mr. Benjamin Snyder: self-described gourmand, novice cookbook author, and—based on his near-constant reminders of his impending trip—ski aficionado. He'd regaled her with details of his lodgings, their proximity to the slopes, and the endless amenities as well as the various celebrities whose visits acted as a ringing endorsement for the Winter Never Wanted to Hear Another Word About It Ski Lodge.

As he waxed prosaic about what was rapidly becoming Winter's least favorite sport, his pelvis shifted forward as if tugged by an invisible string attached to his belt buckle, and with his upper arms held rigidly at his sides, his forearms danced and fluttered at hip level, drawing attention to the area of his anatomy Winter least wanted to consider. His frantic flapping added a startling visual element to each of his one-sided conversations, effectively stunning his audience into silence.

That was on Monday, as she'd battled with romaine, spinach, arugula, and escarole to find the perfect lettuce for his uninspired Leafy Green Salad. He'd only paused his garrulous praises for his accommodations long enough to disparage her choices as either too languid or too vivacious. By the time she'd found the ideal blend of greenery that walked the fine line between sluggish and effusive, she'd learned enough about the ski lodge to launch an ad campaign for it. And that was only the beginning.

On Tuesday, his attention had been torn between frozen desserts and an equipment tutorial that she'd neither asked for nor wanted. The only positive was that he'd at least stayed in the freezer with her to deliver his lesson on the importance of waxing one's skis. True, she could have liberated herself from the chill of the freezer considerably sooner if he'd simply allowed her to work without repeatedly critiquing her efforts while simultaneously exhausting her with instruction on the differences between rub-on, hot, and high-performance waxes, his bizarre gesticulations accentuating his prolixity all the while.

By midweek, she'd stopped being surprised by her client's flair for vacillation and had instead begun preparing for it—at least, as much as possible. It wasn't an easy task anticipating Benjamin's whims. Still, that hadn't stopped her from trying, which is why she'd withheld several plain buns on the not-so-off-chance that her client would decide he didn't like the sesame seeds after all. Of course, now that she was prepared for that eventuality, he'd probably opt for an entire shoot of buns by themselves in their perfectly sesame-seeded glory, rendering both her planning ahead and the last several hours of her assistant's life spent painting shoe-polish grill marks on partially cooked burger patties completely pointless.

"Those look amazing, Peter." She offered the praise she knew Benjamin would never share. "Even if the world will never see them."

"If that's supposed to be the opposite of a jinx, you should have tried it four days ago."

"I'm more likely to double jinx us than anything else. We'll end up spending an extra week working on this while Benjamin calls us from the ski lift, demanding that we perform every task twice."

"Shut your mouth," he howled, eliciting a stunned look from his boss. "You know that I mean that in the most loving and respectful way possible."

"How else would I take it?" She loved working with Peter, and he knew it.

Besides, their suffering at Benjamin's hands was mostly her fault. If she hadn't been so eager to add to her client roster—a move that, in this case, had backfired spectacularly—they would be happily outside of Benjamin's chaotic orbit. Failing that, if she had pushed back at the first sign of his chronic indecision, married to an outsized need for control, the week might have gone a bit more smoothly—either because she got them fired or successfully bypassed her client's more challenging quirks. She could "if only" all day, but the sole remedy to the situation was to focus on her work and try to stay positive.

"We just have to survive the next few hours, and then Aspen can have Benjamin," she offered in small consolation as she pushed one rack of buns to the corner of the commercial kitchen.

"That's the best thing I've heard since *Midnights* came out."

She took a deep, cleansing breath, savoring the smell of freedom, though that might have been the potent combination of hot glue, shoe polish, and Peter's cologne. With a lightness she hadn't felt in days, she launched into a happy dance that looked more like the erratic flapping of a windsock in a hurricane than any movement that could be called dancing. And even though it would give Peter ample fuel for future mocking, she couldn't help but add her own soundtrack, complete with ad-libbed lyrics set to the tune of "Good as Hell."

"I placed the seeds on, glued them well. Buns, how you lookin'? Lookin' good as hell." She shimmed to the beat in her head and allowed herself to belt out the last line, her joy and relief overtaking her.

"You need to write Lizzo a formal apology for bastardizing her material," Peter admonished.

"Pardon me for feeling euphoric."

"About hamburger buns."

"Ignore him. He's just jealous," she said as she again gazed lovingly at her morning's labors. "If I were a burger, I would love to be inside you."

"Are you propositioning your buns?"

Winter leapt at the sound of the voice behind her and spun around to find Macy, the equally long-suffering photographer, slumped in a chair and eyeing her warily. Even her afro looked tired.

"As if you weren't about to do the same thing. Look at these beauties."

"This job has pushed you over the edge."

"You should have been here for the song and dance," Peter called from his side of the kitchen, prompting a raised eyebrow from Macy.

"Is it wrong to love your work?" Winter asked innocently.

"It is when the client is a walking nightmare," Macy answered matter-of-factly.

"He's not that bad." Both of them glared at Winter. "I mean, he's bad. There's no arguing that. But not nightmare bad, more excessively exasperating bad."

"I stand by my wording."

"I stand by her wording too."

"Come on, you guys. Every job has its challenges."

"Does every job have an indecisive dictator who makes each day twice as long as it has to be while also constantly reminding everyone that 'we're on a tight schedule' because he has a ski trip planned?"

"Well, no. I mean, that's a super specific complaint."

"You are too pure for this world," Peter said while Macy favored her with a sympathetic look.

"The snow is starting to accumulate in Aspen, so we need to spend a little less time socializing and a little more time working." Benjamin appeared behind her, his eyes glued to one of the many ski apps he'd been consulting since day one of this job. "Are those for the burgers?" he asked after glancing up long enough to notice his surroundings.

Torn between sarcasm and professionalism, Winter kept her mouth shut and simply waited for whatever blow Benjamin was about to deliver. Behind him, Macy pantomimed strangling their tormentor.

"I'm not sure." He circled the racks, scrutinizing the buns like a school nurse performing a lice check. "They're so perfect."

"Thank you," Winter said, though she should have known better than to misinterpret his comment as praise for her work.

"It sends the wrong message."

She desperately wanted to point out that they were seeds, not semaphores. Not that her words would penetrate the thick miasma of uncertainty that accompanied Benjamin like a storm cloud over everyone else's heads. Instead, she merely stood there silently. Meanwhile, Peter and Macy flanked her like her own security force.

Completely oblivious to the insult he was adding to injury, he continued frowning at the buns. "It's too corporate, don't you think? I'd hate for someone to see the pictures and then run out for a Big Mac instead of using my recipe."

"Your burger isn't even in the same class as a Big Mac," Peter said, earning an elbow to the ribs from his boss.

"Good point, Peter." Benjamin clapped him on the shoulder, a hearty thanks for an insult he'd entirely missed the point of. "But just to be on the safe side, you can remove all these seeds for the pictures, can't you? That won't take long, will it? We're on a tight schedule."

"No time at all," Winter assured him, her smile never faltering.

Through clenched teeth, Macy said, "We'll get started on that. Why don't you go check on your flight?"

"Great idea." Benjamin immediately whipped out his phone, and as the chatter about airports, wind speeds, and turbulence launched, his arms flailing overtime, Peter nudged him toward the far end of the set where poor Laura, his harried and largely superfluous art director, awaited the next blow to her ego.

"If they've already bought the book, what does it matter if they never use the recipes?" Macy asked as soon as he was out of earshot. "He's already got their money at that point."

"Not to mention that no one needs a cookbook to make a hamburger." Peter joined the commiserating. "What next? A guide to peanut butter and jelly sandwiches? A how-to on a bowl of cereal?"

"And some other team of unfortunate artists to help him sell it," Macy said.

"Amen to that." Peter picked up one of the buns Winter had so lovingly adorned and frowned at it. "How are we supposed to deseed these without destroying them? This will take all day."

"Not unless you want another time management lecture from Captain Clueless. We're on a tight schedule, remember?" Macy reminded him.

Peter growled. "This is so infuriating."

"It's really not worth getting all worked up about this, guys." Winter moved the offending buns to one side of the kitchen. She wouldn't discard them until the shoot officially wrapped, but she also didn't want to keep tripping over the reminder of a morning wasted.

"Beg to differ, boss. That man is evil and needs to be stopped before he drives some innocent young assistant to commit murder on his entirely too forgiving boss's behalf."

"You don't have to villainize Benjamin just to make me feel better."

"What if we're doing it to make ourselves feel better?" Macy asked.

"By all means, carry on, but I plan to keep working and maybe get us out of here faster." At that, Winter unveiled her reserve rack of plain buns.

Macy gasped. "You beautiful genius. If we survive this day, we need to go out for the biggest drinks this city can pour."

"I know the perfect place," Peter said, an unnerving twinkle in his eye.

Too many hours later, Winter walked through the front door of The Ski Shop, a bar whose name couldn't have been a more fitting end to this week. She'd made a pit stop at her hotel to wash the horrors of the day off her. Not that she wasn't eager to let a giant glass of shiraz erase the past week from her memory, but thanks to Benjamin's frustratingly hands-on approach, she'd ended up with the barbecue sauce version of the Rorschach test on the front of her sweater. She'd treated the stain immediately, but she knew in her heart that the sweater was a goner. And while she could technically place the blame for a beloved cozy top's untimely demise at Benjamin's feet, really, shame on her for wearing cream-colored anything to work.

Despite her delay and her impatience to put the past week behind her, she'd opted to take the subway to the out-of-the-way bar Peter had suggested. And while she'd enjoyed a much-needed chance to regroup during the train ride, she'd also missed her stop and ended up walking several blocks in the frigid temperatures. She'd pulled her coat more tightly around her as an arctic wind whipped her hair to-and-fro, leaving her looking like the redheaded version of a bowerbird's nest. By the time another gust pushed her into the bar's entryway, her face and hands were frozen, and any effort she'd put into her appearance had been spectacularly undone. Still, as she reached for the door handle, she felt curiously hopeful.

As soon as she opened the door, the indistinct susurration of multiple simultaneous conversations flowed out onto the street. She was pleasantly surprised at the size of the crowd. She hadn't been expecting so many people to be out on a frigid night in February, but apparently she'd underestimated the quirky appeal of The Ski Shop. And she was more than happy to take the popularity of the bar as a ringing endorsement of an establishment that by all appearances was little more than an afterthought, like the owner of the place suddenly remembered they had a bar to run and had haphazardly gathered the necessary furnishings.

A quick glance around told her that every surface was what could politely be called well-worn. She didn't see any matching chairs at any of the tables or in the entire bar for that matter, like there had been a buy-twenty-get-twenty-free sale on mismatched furniture. The tables sat at varying heights and represented the full range of geometric possibilities. It was a complete hodgepodge of seating choices.

As she scanned the space for her friends, she was oddly disappointed to find that The Ski Shop was just a bar with an unusual name. Where she'd expected to find an abundance of ski-themed décor, she merely found a few haphazardly placed paper snowflakes that could just as easily be the bar's standard furnishings as leftover holiday decorations, a theory supported by the limp strands of garland framing the mirror behind the bar.

A chalkboard to the right of the bar hyped the daily specials, including the Negronski and the Faceplant—two cocktails with an intimidating amount of alcohol—as well as a smattering of curious food options, the most notable of which had to be the Schuss-kebabs. Lamentably, a flyer heralding tonight's karaoke event hung on the board, and Winter's empathy kicked up a notch in anticipation of several strangers' impending public humiliation. The bar itself stretched the full length of one wall, and patrons lined up two deep, eager either for overpriced novelty drinks or the inebriation required to survive an evening of truly terrible covers.

Winter made her way through the crowd, swerving to avoid oblivious patrons whose booming conversations presumably required wild gesturing. She narrowly avoided intimate knowledge of one young man's fist as he made a particularly monumental point about a band Winter had never heard of—though to be fair, it could have been a sports team that she was equally in the dark about.

Despite the crush of people, Winter managed to find her friends near the back of the bar, crowded around two round tables that had been pushed together. Laura spotted her first and squealed a hello that drew half the bar's attention. She jumped up from her seat and hugged Winter like they were old friends who had spent the last decade apart rather than work acquaintances who'd met five days earlier and parted not an hour before.

"Someone got an early start." Winter disentangled herself from Laura's viselike grasp.

"I'm having a placefant." She shook her head and tried again. "Faceplant," she said with the extra care often taken by those who were sober enough to know that they were drunk but drunk enough to think they could mask their inebriation with deliberate speech.

"And what have you eaten today?"

"I swallowed my pride. Does that count?"

"Sadly, no."

She steered Laura back to her seat, with its comforting illusion of security if not the real thing, and looked to her friends for help. Unfortunately, Macy was engrossed in the vital task of selecting a song for karaoke. To her credit, she'd embraced the mission wholeheartedly, as evidenced by her handwritten list of possibilities, each with a sub-list of pros and cons. Meanwhile, Peter was distracting both himself and their waiter from the human PSA for sobriety currently extracting every ounce of sustenance from the booze-soaked fruit in her otherwise depleted glass.

Scanning the three-page menu, Winter found two and a half pages of alcohol plus a small list of appetizers, none of which were up to the task of doing battle with the quart of liquor currently presiding over Laura's sensibilities. The gondola of fries was looking suddenly impressive if she wanted to prevent her friend from living up to her drink's name. She knew that her chances of getting that train back in the station were slim, but she had to at least try to curb Laura's impending morning of regret. She also knew that she didn't have the luxury of time, so waiting for Peter to relinquish his sway over their server was not an option.

"I'll be back," she said to anyone who might have been listening and fought her way back through the crowd to the bar.

She snagged a stool on the end of the bar closest to the door and made herself comfortable. Or, at least as comfortable as one could be on a barstool that rocked from side to side whenever she adjusted her position. It was a little like when her mom let her ride the coin-operated horse outside of Whitlock's Grocery Store but with the added possibility of humiliating herself once alcohol was introduced to the equation. The bar itself was sticky and slightly damp in places, a result of the busyness of the staff rather than a commentary on the cleanliness of the establishment. Two young men and one woman worked behind the bar, pouring beers and mixing drinks, their speed and professionalism impressive. Winter found herself entertained by the way they spun and maneuvered around one another, almost like a ballet.

As she waited her turn to order, she felt more than saw someone drop into the seat beside her. Judging by the heavy sigh that filled the air between them, Winter expected to find another refugee from Benjamin's cookbook shoot. When she turned to see her neighbor, her jaw dropped.

She'd know that face anywhere—the determined jawline, the porcelain skin marred by one small mole on the right cheek, bright hazel eyes alert to her surroundings. Even with the messy bob in place of her long black hair, there was no mistaking the woman beside her—Avery Sumner, Winter's first crush and the root source of most of her teenage awkwardness.

"No way," she muttered.

"Excuse me?"

"Uh, I said, rough day?"

"Hopefully it won't be for much longer."

CHAPTER THREE

It took an embarrassing length of time for Winter's mouth to close. Initially, she couldn't move past her shock that the universe was toying with her like this—if she had encountered Avery Sumner at any time other than the culmination of the worst week of her professional life, she might have thought she'd won the belated schoolgirl crush lottery. But now, considering all she'd endured in the past five days? There was no way this chance encounter would amount to anything good when so much else had gone so horribly awry. Unless she was being compensated for her suffering, but she didn't really believe that the powers that be worked like that.

But she couldn't unload all that on Avery. Not only would this be the first conversation they'd had outside of Winter's wishful thinking, but if she said everything that she was thinking, it would probably also be their last. Winter was really hoping to make a better first impression than that. Not that she stood much chance of making a good impression now that she'd spent an eon and a half silently staring at Avery, her mouth agape. She had to say something before Avery backed away slowly, avoiding eye contact.

As another gift from the universe, a bartender, whose impressive musculature was only rivaled by his expansive handlebar mustache, intruded upon them, bringing a blissful end to the awkwardness of the moment. He eschewed the pesky formality of taking Avery's order, instead simply bringing her a pint. "Anything else?"

The ease with which he addressed Avery was almost insulting, like he was intentionally pointing out Winter's total lack of composure. Though, to be fair, he probably hadn't spent his entire freshman year of high school pining for her.

"Whatever she's having."

Both Avery and the bartender looked to Winter, and in spite of their full-scale attention aimed directly at her, she found the words she needed.

"That's very nice of you, but—"

"Or maybe it's just pragmatic."

"How so?"

"If you don't order now, you might not get another chance."

"She's not wrong," the muscle-bound mustache confirmed.

"And how is that pragmatic for you?"

"I need the points." She held up her credit card, as if that explained everything. "I've almost earned a twenty-dollar statement credit."

"Maybe you should buy a round for the bar then. Aim high."

"I would, but then they'd all want to thank me, and really, I think I'd rather just talk to you." She shrugged almost shyly, her easy grin selling the innocence of her statement.

Winter fought the rising blush warming her cheeks. Avery Sumner flirting with her? This was so not happening. "Well, then, I'll have a Negronski, a sidecar, one shiraz, four waters, an order of Schuss-kebabs, and some fries."

"Stockpiling for later? Or are you expecting a booze shortage?"

"I like to keep my options open." Winter shrugged and tried to act innocent. She wasn't about to let Avery supply the next round for her work friends, but she did have a point about the service being about as reliable as paper galoshes.

The bartender looked to Avery for approval, his mustache gloriously twitching all the while.

"You heard the lady."

He nodded once, his interest lukewarm at best, then drifted away to take care of Winter's order.

"I'm Avery, by the way." She shook Winter's hand, and despite the chill lingering on Avery's fingers, Winter felt suddenly warm.

"I know," she said and instantly cringed. Three seconds into her first not-imaginary conversation with Avery and she was sending out stalker vibes.

"Have we already met?"

"Not entirely." Wishing she could erase the last thirty seconds of her life, Winter scrunched up her face in an expression that she hoped was disarming and apologetic but probably only amped up the creep factor.

And just like that, she was fourteen years old again, gangly, awkward, and all too ready to overcompensate for her shortcomings with over-the-top friendliness. Despite her outgoing nature, she'd never managed to work up the courage to talk to Avery, who had always been cool and gorgeous and completely out of her league. Back then, Avery's personality had bridged all of the social strata at Anneville High. Her charm and good looks were impervious to the restrictions of cliques, which made her oddly even less approachable to Winter.

But it wasn't like she would get a second second chance. Reminding herself that she wasn't a clumsy teenager any longer, she decided to make the best of the opportunity.

"Maybe you just look like an Avery." Winter tried to remedy her blunder.

"Does anyone *look* like an Avery?" Her tone was, thankfully, more amused than insulted.

"I'm sorry. Can you forget I spoke?"

"Why would I want to do something like that?"

"To prevent my death by mortification?"

"I didn't realize the consequences were so dire." Avery winked before taking a sip of her drink, a smile evident around her glass.

How Winter hadn't managed to completely blow this opportunity she had no idea, but she supposed she still had time.

"I still don't know your name. Or how you knew mine." Avery narrowed her hazel eyes in mock suspicion, and Winter resisted the urge to say that she'd tell her but then she'd have to kill her. She'd already dug herself a deep enough hole.

"I'm Winter."

"And?" Avery raised her eyebrows, a clear request for the answer to her other question, an answer Winter wasn't sure she wanted to give just yet.

"And I'm happy to officially meet you."

Their eyes locked again, and Winter wondered what alternate universe she'd stepped into to find Avery Sumner not only talking to her but apparently enjoying the experience. She was even more gorgeous now than in high school, which seemed impossible. Winter stared into those large, bright eyes that she'd admired from a distance so many years before, not really believing what was happening. The rest of the bar fell away, and Winter couldn't help the grin that blossomed at her spontaneous memories of Avery. Her fourteen-year-old self would never believe that this conversation was happening, much less that Winter had maintained her composure, more or less.

When the bartender appeared with Winter's impressive order, the spell they were under dissipated. Their hands fell apart and their eye contact broke, but otherwise, neither of them moved. Neither touched her drink, the silence stretched between them charged with possibility.

"This is a catastrophe of the highest order."

She heard Peter's voice behind her and immediately lamented her assistant's flair for the dramatic. He was like an attention-seeking missile, and the last thing she wanted or needed in this moment was Peter's input on the woman currently acting as the most welcome of distractions.

"Macy is insisting on singing 'Son of a Preacher Man,' and you're off doing god knows what instead of helping me convince her to pick something from this century." He stopped abruptly, an all-too-eager grin taking over his face. "Suddenly it all makes sense."

"What does?"

"Your prolonged absence." Peter smiled more broadly at Avery and offered the least subtle wink in the history of facial expressions.

"For your information, the service is slow. If you don't believe me, just ask your new boyfriend." She hitched her chin at the waiter whose attention had been so focused on Peter earlier.

"Slow or advantageous?"

"It's certainly worked in my favor," Avery quipped, fueling Peter's sass.

Instead of trying to match Avery's flirtatious confidence, Winter rose from her seat and began collecting the drinks she'd ordered. With one hand on her shoulder, Peter pushed her back into her seat and, eyebrow raised, took the drinks from her hands.

"What kind of assistant would I be if I didn't encourage this tryst?"

"The kind who still has a job in the morning."

He merely scoffed at her empty threat. "You'd be lost without me. And in case I wasn't clear, you are officially excused from our soiree."

"What about Macy's song?"

"You're sitting beside this"—he looked from Winter to Avery and back again—"and you're concerned about Macy's karaoke debut? Sometimes I question your priorities."

"I like him," Avery chimed in.

"That's because you don't know him."

"I'll make your excuses to Macy. You make sure there's something to excuse."

Winter shook her head as Peter sauntered away, his victory clear. But she couldn't exactly complain about spending more time with Avery, who wasn't even trying to hide her smile.

"He deserves a raise," she said.

"I'll take it under advisement."

Somewhere behind them, a perky-voiced woman commanded the attention of the rest of the patrons, welcoming them to karaoke night at The Ski Shop. The smattering of applause was about what Winter would expect from a crowd whose night out had been hijacked by the possibility of enduring the off-key warbling of strangers. As the first performer launched into an enthusiastic but ultimately ill-advised version of a hit pop song from a few years earlier, Avery's smile fell.

"Do you want to get out of here?"

"And do what?"

"We could take a walk."

"It's twelve degrees outside."

"I could promise not to let you get too cold." The boldness of that line was at odds with Avery's unassuming expression.

"And how would you keep such a promise?"

"Do they not have hot cocoa where you're from?"

"The best in the Midwest, but it's not me I'm worried about."

"Then you could promise not to let me get cold." Avery's grin suggested a playful innocence.

Every way in which this was a bad idea raced through Winter's head. What impression was she giving this woman? She hardly knew Avery. What if she was a charming serial killer looking for her next victim? It made zero sense to follow her out of a public place to her doom. And even if, as was most likely the case, Avery wasn't the female Ted Bundy, was it really worth risking hypothermia just to spend a little more time with her? Especially since there was no logical reason that they couldn't just stay at the bar, where they were warm and where drinks were somewhat accessible. Quite simply, there was no good excuse to go off with Avery.

"You're on." In clear defiance of her brain, Winter's mouth trundled carelessly ahead, saying the exact opposite of what it should have. But the look of surprised delight on Avery's face reassured her, if only a little.

Against Winter's protests, Avery insisted on paying the bill, including the round of drinks for the table that Winter had abandoned. Then she helped Winter into her coat and held the door open for her. Either she was a well-mannered serial killer, or maybe Winter would be completely safe, aside from certain frostbite.

CHAPTER FOUR

One or two pedestrians rushed past, their puffy coats and hurried strides a testament to the folly of this adventure. The noise of the city had faded away, surrounding them in the boundless silence of frigid winter nights, when a hushed wonder blankets the world. If not for the frosty air and rampant light pollution, it would be a perfect night for dreamily stargazing. In short, the night was magically still, a wondrous effect that Winter attributed to the nearness of Avery rather than the likelihood that people were simply avoiding the cold.

As they walked, their pace somewhat leisurely in spite of the arctic temperatures, Winter's body acclimated to the weather, and she allowed herself to enjoy the exhilarating nearness of the woman beside her, who had yet to point them in the direction of any location less oblique than "not The Ski Shop." Their shoulders grazed as they headed east. Or maybe south. In all honesty, Winter's awareness of anything other than her companion had fled the scene long ago, and she'd been operating on lust and impulse since Avery entered the bar. They could be walking to Wisconsin or circling The Ski Shop for all

Winter knew. Nor was she particularly invested in where this journey took them, but given the size of the city they currently traversed, she supposed it might be best to determine a goal of some sort before hypothermia set in.

"What's next on the agenda?"

"What would you like to do?"

"I thought the walk was the activity."

"It doesn't have to be." Avery stopped and shook her head. "I just heard how that sounded. I promise I didn't mean it that way."

"Is it wrong that I'm suddenly more comfortable with you now that you've accidentally propositioned me?"

"You're cute when you gibe." They walked in silence for a moment, the wind having its way with Winter's hair. "What would you like to do?"

"This is your town. You tell me."

"We could go somewhere for a drink," Avery said.

"We just left somewhere that had plenty of drinks."

"But I hijacked you before you even got to taste your wine."

"I don't need alcohol to enjoy your company."

"That's a relief. Are you hungry? We could grab a bite somewhere."

Winter shuddered at the thought of coming face-to-face with anything even remotely reminiscent of Benjamin and his accursed cookbook. "I'm kind of over food for the time being."

"Should I ask?"

"It's probably better if you don't."

"Forget food, then. There are hundreds of things we can do that don't involve eating."

"*Hundreds* of things?" Winter asked with playful incredulity.

"Shocking, I know, but it's true. I've been keeping track of all the things to do here."

At some point as they walked, Avery had slipped her hand into Winter's, a subtle yet confident move that had Winter questioning reality.

"Like a recreation compendium," Winter suggested with a calm in clear defiance of her racing heart.

"Exactly."

"It sounds like a big project. You must have started it as soon as you moved here."

"How do you know I'm not originally from here?"

"That's classified." She winked awkwardly but stopped short of cringing at herself. Somehow, her gawkiness seemed to come off as charming rather than off-putting to Avery. If only she'd known at age fourteen that Avery found a complete lack of smoothness so enticing.

"More from that secret file you have on me?" She smiled, seemingly unconcerned about a complete stranger's surplus of knowledge on her.

Winter's only response was to shrug in what she hoped was a disarming way. She watched in relief as Avery's smile grew, and their eyes locked again. The air between them buzzed, and their already glacial pace slowed until they stopped completely, narrowly avoiding a collision with a woman so thoroughly engrossed in her cell phone that she scarcely offered an irritated grunt as she brushed past. In the wake of that brusque encounter, Avery stepped back, her foot slipping on a patch of ice and sending her tumbling to the ground. Winter helped her up, the electricity between them reigniting when they touched. They both shivered, whether from the cold or from the intimacy of the moment, she wasn't sure.

Gently, Avery rubbed Winter's shoulders, arousing a fresh wave of chills. "Why don't we discuss our options over hot cocoa."

Twenty minutes later, they sat at a small table in a cozy shop that seemed to specialize in decadence. In addition to a staggering assortment of hot cocoas, the menu offered an impressive array of desserts—including several ice cream concoctions that Winter looked forward to sampling in warmer months—plus espresso drinks, beer, and wine. She carefully sipped her classic cocoa, trying desperately not to wear the evidence of her indulgence on her face or clothing. Across the table, Avery warmed her hands on her mug, watching as Winter navigated the mountain of whipped cream atop her beverage.

"We could go ice-skating?" Avery passed her a napkin but thankfully said nothing about the whipped cream dotting Winter's nose. "Or bumper cars? We could go to the Empire State Building. I know it sounds touristy, but you are a tourist."

"I did live here for five years."

"Here? At this very table?"

"In Brooklyn," Winter corrected, pretending to be exasperated but enjoying Avery's playful mood.

"So this is your city too." Avery's smile reached her eyes.

"This was never my city." Winter exhaled sharply, remembering the hardship of her time in New York.

"Is that why you left?"

She shook her head, wondering how much to share. As a rule, heartbreak wasn't ideal conversation for a date, or whatever this was. She didn't know Avery, not really, and she wasn't obligated to reveal all her secrets. But she also had yet to reveal much about herself to Avery, giving her kind of an unfair advantage. Ultimately, she opted for the simple, if somewhat vague, truth.

"My family needed me."

"And that worked?"

"You wouldn't go home for your family?"

"This is home," she answered tersely.

"Well, my dad was dying, so that made it an easy decision."

Avery suddenly found her cocoa fascinating. Conversely, Winter lost all interest in her beverage. She busied herself with people watching, an easy distraction thanks to the diversity of patrons crowding the space. It seemed everyone from kids who probably should have been in bed to youths with an impressive array of unnatural hair colors on display appreciated the heavenly properties of hot chocolate. Behind Avery, a pair of ladies—whose matching halos of frizzy white hair suggested they shared either genes or a subpar hairdresser—partook of conversation and a slice of pie.

"I'm sorry about your dad." Avery's soft voice penetrated Winter's thoughts. "Do you want to get out of here?"

"I'd love to."

Again holding hands, they walked in silence for several minutes, Avery occasionally offering a supportive squeeze.

Winter had no idea how far they'd walked or in what direction when Avery broke the silence.

"Do you ever think about moving back?"

"Sometimes I miss the city—all the activity, and nights like this." She looked to Avery, thinking that things like this never happened in Anneville. "But I love so many things about my little town. That's home for me." Avery nodded but remained silent. She looked almost defeated. "I do end up here for work a lot. Maybe we can plan ahead for the next time I'm here."

"I'd like that."

Avery offered to make sure Winter returned to her hotel safely, and not wanting to say good night any time soon, Winter happily accepted. The remainder of the walk passed mostly in comfortable silence. She felt the chill of the night creeping past her coat, and her gloves had stopped being effective several blocks earlier. Even so, she lamented how quickly they arrived at her hotel. She thought she might have walked with Avery all night and still been sad when the rising sun brought their time together to a close.

They stepped out of the cold and into the lobby, where Peter and Macy had conspicuously gathered. Winter would have frowned at them or tried to shoo them away, but that only would have made the situation worse.

"I should probably get your number, so we can start that planning." Avery smiled disarmingly.

Even if Winter hadn't wanted to share her phone number, how could she not in the face of such charm? Calling herself "Winter (Woman of Mystery)," she added her number to Avery's contacts then kissed her cheek and turned toward her ridiculously cheerful friends. With a promise to be in touch, Avery headed back out into the frigid night.

Before her friends even had the chance to ask for details, her phone pinged with an incoming text.

Too soon? Avery asked.

Definitely not, she thought, celebrating her incredible luck.

CHAPTER FIVE

Although Winter traveled regularly for work, spending time in cities both glamorous and not, the town she loved most was her hometown. Anneville was unlike any other place she'd ever been, not only because of its size—which, even by the most generous standards of measurement, amounted to just under two square miles—but also because of the people who called Anneville home.

Not long ago, she would have cited those same people as her principal reason for fleeing the town. With a collective worldview about as expansive as razor wire, they'd made life for young queer Winter uncomfortable, to say the least. But sometime between her departure for college and her return a decade later, the town had transformed. Now, as she walked the curved streets of her little hamlet, cars passing at a leisurely twenty miles per hour, she was as likely to encounter a Pride flag as she was to see a bumper sticker proclaiming some parent's pride in their honor roll student.

This afternoon as she strolled toward the Anneville Shopping Plaza, enjoying a rare, brief moment where her obligations weren't constantly vying for her attention, Winter savored the peculiar appeal of her small town. On a map, Anneville wasn't much. In fact, all through her childhood, it hadn't even shown up on most maps, dwarfed as it was by neighboring cities whose populations climbed well above the few hundred inhabitants of Anneville. It wasn't until high school, when she and the other members of the cartography club—a club she joined more out of misguided sympathy for her oft-forgotten neighbor Jacob Tompkins than any great love of maps—campaigned to get official acknowledgment for their tiny town, that people outside of the immediate area began to recognize Anneville. By then, of course, Google Maps made all of their hard work, not to mention the club itself, more or less obsolete.

Large, soft snowflakes began to drift down around her, a welcome bit of seasonally appropriate ornamentation and exactly Winter's favorite way to experience her town. With Valentine's Day fast approaching, cupids and hearts dotted the landscape, though, in what was perhaps a more salacious effect than had been intended, the immense, love-hungry cherubs leering from lampposts around town appeared more lewd than the city council had hoped for. Perhaps, with Mother Nature's help, the snow would dim Cupid's more suggestive qualities.

For now, it collected on the ground and blanketed the duplexes that lined either side of the curved streets she strolled. With few exceptions, every home in town was a duplex, meaning residents lived in extremely close proximity to one another, a condition that fueled gossip—essentially the GDP of Anneville. Rampant confabulation notwithstanding, the nearness of neighbors had benefited her more than once, especially during her parents' respective illnesses.

Shoving those unpleasant memories to the side, she shifted her focus to the recent spate of activity in her normally mundane life. She'd been home from New York for just over a week and had yet to experience any downtime. From meticulous prep work for upcoming jobs, to the monthly meeting of the Special Events Committee, of which she was co-chair, to aligning her holiday décor with the calendar, to her current task of meeting her friends Gabe and Noah to finalize plans for their Valentine's Day event, she'd had almost no time to focus on what she really wanted to do—which was basically a deep dive into all things Avery.

In the brief yet seemingly endless time she'd been home, they'd texted a handful of times, basically, enough to keep her hopes up and send her dashing for her phone every time it chimed, but not so much that she seemed desperate. She hoped. Fun, flirty, and lighthearted was the tone she wanted to establish—in clear defiance of her signature awkwardness. Having somehow managed not to scare Avery off with her near-stalker antics during their chance encounter, she intended to capitalize on this admittedly frustrating opportunity. Sure, she'd love to get to know Avery better in person, preferably over a series of cozy rendezvous, but Winter had to admit that texting had certain advantages, chief among them time to reflect and minimize her embarrassment.

By the time she reached the bar, her cheeks were numb, and she'd tested the limitations of her so-called waterproof boots. Though she was thirsty and surprisingly toasty thanks to an overabundance of apparel, she stopped just outside to admire the bar.

All through her childhood, The Anneville Tap had seemed magical. Every adult she knew spent time at The Tap, and preteen Winter knew it had to be some elegant oasis. What a disappointment, then, to sneak in as a seventeen-year-old with delusions of sophistication and discover the utter lack of refinement in the cracked linoleum floors and smoke-tinged walls.

To see it now, after Noah's transformation, the bar was even more spectacular than what she'd always imagined it might be. She couldn't believe it when he bought the bar—she was certain he was throwing money away. The Anneville Tap would never be more than a neighborhood watering hole, a dive where the proximity to home held as much allure as the bargain-basement beer prices. But under Noah's management, the space had gradually shifted from the dumpster of bars to the crown jewel of downtown Anneville.

She hadn't even removed her scarf before she was ambushed from both sides and found herself in the middle of the warmest embrace from Gabe and Noah. Within minutes, she was deposited at their favorite table—the one in the rear with a view of the entire bar. Noah disappeared behind the bar while Gabe offered the rundown of all the latest happenings in town, which amounted to a surprising number of sledding accidents for an entirely flat town. By the time Winter divested herself of the bulk of her layers, Noah joined them at the table, tray full of spectacularly garnished red and pink cocktails in hand.

"Isn't this why you have a staff?" Winter selected a garnet-colored drink, admiring both its color and its imaginative coral tuile garnish.

"No, I have a staff to keep me company when Gabe is occupied." They clinked glasses, and Winter took a tentative sip of her valentine cocktail. "Plus, I like it when they call me king."

"I never should have let you take my last name." Gabe hid a smile behind his drink.

"Because you really wanted to be Gabriel Niedlander."

"I just wanted to be with you." They exchanged a sweetly loving glance that signaled Winter's rapid transition to third-wheel status.

"Tell me about the event," she said, interrupting their impending mating ritual.

"You're going to love it. I had the best idea ever." Noah applauded his own genius, and Winter couldn't help but get caught up in his excitement. Even if his brilliant idea ended up being the Valentine's Day equivalent of leaded gasoline, she was ready to support it.

"Wait," Gabe said. "Don't we need to ask—"

"Right, right, right. I'm getting ahead of myself again."

Despite their obvious eagerness to consult Winter on some important matter, neither man actually got around to looping her in. Instead, they spent several minutes chattering amongst themselves about the need to ask without ever getting to the asking part of the conversation.

"Will one of you please just ask me?"

Noah slapped his forehead while Gabe rolled his eyes at himself, and then, without warning, they simultaneously asked, "Who are you bringing?"

"Who am I bringing?" she repeated, hoping to find some clarity in repetition.

"Who's your date?" Gabe asked.

"I was going to bring Miss Opal. She doesn't get out as much as she used to. I think it would be fun for her." Winter looked forward to spending an evening out with her neighbor, who always had the best advice, gossip, and stories.

"It's Valentine's Day weekend. Don't you even want to pretend to be interested in romance?"

"I'm not not interested," she protested.

"Then you're open to meeting our friend." Gabe offered a Cheshire cat grin but stopped short of rubbing his hands together.

"I'm open to supporting my friends. That's it." As if to remind herself why she wasn't interested in any blind date the boys had to offer, she checked her phone for any communication from Avery.

"What's wrong with just meeting someone?" Noah asked.

"It's just not the right time," she said, still not looking up from her phone.

"Really?" Gabe asked. "Because it hasn't been the right time for a while now. And I'm thinking that if we leave it up to you, it will never be the right time."

"And if I left it up to you, there would never be a wrong time. Or person. No thank you."

"Eyes up here." Gabe used his teacher voice and covered her phone with his hand. "What's so interesting about your phone?"

"Nothing," she answered too quickly and slid the offending device back into her pocket, but it was too late. Gabe's mouth fell open, and his eyes practically doubled in size.

"You met someone, didn't you?"

She considered denying it. After all, she and Avery weren't exactly an item. One incredible night and a few dozen follow-up texts didn't exactly mean that Winter was off the market for good. But she was dying to share this news with someone.

"It's not anything, really, but I sort of ran into Avery Sumner in New York."

"Tell me everything, and please let this story have a steamy ending."

"I kissed her cheek. Does that count?"

"That's not even room temperature," he complained. "When the universe hands you a gift, you're supposed to open it. And by 'open it,' I mean—"

"We all know what you mean." She took a sip of her violently red drink and considered how to explain what she was feeling. "There are so many reasons this won't work out, not the least of which is the nine hundred or so miles between us. But I don't want to give up on it before it even starts, if that makes sense." She shrugged, hoping her friends would understand and respect her need for time. Gabe smiled and held her hands, his support clear.

"I told you we should have just sprung it on her." Noah fell back in his seat, defeated.

CHAPTER SIX

Winter had never seen The Tap bursting with so much activity, and while she'd like to take credit for luring patrons with her eye-catching holiday decorations—her gifts with crepe paper and tissue paper pom-poms were unparalleled—she knew that the real draw was the theme for the event: My Furry Valentine. In a stroke of business and philanthropic genius, Noah had invited human and animal representatives from various shelters to the bar, making The Anneville Tap appealing to all, regardless of relationship status. As she meandered through the bar, she saw her special events committee cochair Beulah Singer and her husband bonding with a basset hound from Lazy Lucy's Senior Pet Sanctuary. Without hesitation, she veered in the opposite direction lest Beulah's events antennae rise, ensnaring her in a lengthy and ultimately pointless discussion of the still unsettled but vitally important Festival of Anns—the signature event on the overfull special events calendar. There'd be time enough to debate the finer points of the city's anniversary blowout once this evening's festivities were complete.

Farther on, her high school gym teacher, Miss Clark, dressed in her traditional velour tracksuit—this one in festive pink—doted on a charming tuxedo cat from Makin' Muffins Cat Rescue—a picture-perfect pairing if ever Winter saw one. All around her, people connected with potential companions, whether canine, feline, or human, and her heart warmed at the sight. The drawback, however, was the vicariousness of her delight. Yes, she was truly happy for her fellow Annevillians and all the animals who were finding their forever homes, but she couldn't help the twinge of jealousy that dampened her joy.

Challenging though it was, she resisted the urge to spend the rest of the night as a bed for one of the potential adoptees. After all, she wasn't there to cuddle up to one of the furry visitors, no matter how enticing the idea was. She was there to help her friends and avoid being set up with Bachelorette Number Twelve. Although she did appreciate the sentiment behind the boys' semiregular matchmaking, she just wished they weren't quite so averse to taking a hint. It was like a chronic allergy.

She made two loops around the bar, a somewhat challenging feat, given the many obstacles in the form of patrons, employees, volunteers, and cuddly critters occupying the space. As she made her rounds, she gathered empty glasses, chatted with friends and neighbors who weren't otherwise occupied, and masterfully dodged Beulah. Congratulating herself for a job well done, she allowed herself to drift closer to the rescue activity lining the periphery of the bar. Much to her delight, the first adoptee to catch her eye happened to be an utterly adorable white and brown pit bull puppy. As he wagged his tail, which, in turn, wagged his entire body, his floppy ears bounced and flapped, beckoning her to him. How could she resist such an invitation?

"You are too cute to be real," Winter squealed and dropped to the floor for a closer look. A warm pink tongue slapped her nose in greeting.

"This is Basil," the woman at the other end of the leash said. Her name tag identified her as Joy, a volunteer from Pittie-ful Pups.

She smiled at her charge and then at Winter—a smile that not only reached her dark eyes, but also made them twinkle.

The aptly named Joy towered over Winter and Basil, a fact that would remain even if Winter could free herself from the puppy's enthusiastic hellos long enough to stand beside the statuesque brunette.

Winter wanted to ask about more about Basil—more out of politeness than because she harbored any illusions that she could provide him the home he deserved—but any time she tried to speak, Basil's tongue wound up in her mouth.

"You'll have to forgive him. This is his first event, and he's still learning his manners." Joy gently tugged the leash, giving Winter a reprieve from Basil's exuberant greeting.

"I don't think that will hurt his chances any," Winter said. "He's got me half-convinced that I should take him home with me tonight."

"What's holding you back?" Joy asked.

"Mostly concern for Basil's welfare," Winter answered honestly. At Joy's quizzical expression, she explained, "I travel a lot for work."

"There's always boarding. Or a dog sitter," she countered. "And is there a better homecoming than a greeting like this?" As if on cue, Basil wiggled himself into Winter's lap and resumed his vigorous face licking.

Her audience effectively captive, Joy launched into an impressive sales pitch, touting Basil's many fine qualities, most of which pertained to his affability and overall cuteness. "He hasn't mastered many commands yet," she confessed, "but he's only four months old, and he's incredibly smart. He'll get it down in no time."

As she spoke, something on the other side of the bar caught her eye. The inventory of Basil's attributes slowed, offering Winter an opportunity to speak.

"I'm sure he's the best puppy in the world, but believe me when I say he's better off without me." The volunteer nodded but kept her gaze locked on whatever had captured her attention. "I really don't have the best track record for keeping things alive."

Joy's head snapped back. At her wide-eyed concern, Winter explained.

"I killed a cactus," she offered sheepishly. "And those are supposed to be hearty plants. They can survive in the desert, but one month with me, and it's curtains. I just don't think I'm ready for more advanced forms of life."

"I see your point." Joy laughed, but her focus was already back on the other side of the room.

Naturally curious, Winter followed Joy's gaze all the way to the familiar profile of a petite blonde trapped in conversation with Judge Richards and her parrot.

"Great. Now I'm not even as interesting as a bird."

"I'm sorry. I just think she's amazing."

"Robin? Or the parrot?"

Joy spun around, her full attention on Winter. "You know her?"

"Robin, yes. The parrot? Not so much. Would you like me to introduce you?"

"I'm supposed to meet someone—Gabe told me he had a friend he wanted to introduce me to. Do you think it's her?"

Winter was ninety-five percent sure that she was the friend in question, but Joy didn't need to know that. "Let's find out." She reluctantly removed the wiggly puppy from her lap and rose. He immediately began licking Joy's cheek. "You watch Basil. I'll take care of introductions."

"But I—"

"You'll be fine."

"I don't know what to say."

"Why don't you let Basil help you with that?"

Winter hadn't gotten more than twenty feet away before bumping into a far-too-pleased-with-himself Gabe.

"I see you met Joy. What do you think? Isn't she great?"

"She's very nice," Winter admitted.

"And not unattractive for a lady." His smirk was particularly exasperating, more so than usual. "You could do worse than a not unattractive animal-loving do-gooder who just happens to be single."

"Not for long."

"You've already sealed the deal? I thought this would be harder."

"Don't congratulate yourself just yet, Cupid. Joy is interested in someone else. And, in case you forgot, I'm also interested in someone else."

"First of all, you're interested in someone who lives a thousand miles away."

"Obviously, it's not a perfect situation."

"Last I heard, there was no situation. Unless hypothermia and an extreme lack of kissing count as reasons to put your life on hold." She didn't even get the chance for a rebuttal. "They don't. And second, we put this plan in motion before we knew about your non-thing with Avery."

"Then I can sort of forgive you. And if you'll excuse me, I have some matchmaking to do."

CHAPTER SEVEN

Despite a strong desire to stay home, hunker down under some blankets, and spend the night with thoughts of Avery, Winter made herself attend the monthly joint meeting of the Anneville Special Events Committee and the Anneville Beautification Committee, of which she was the co-chair and vice president, respectively. It had been just over two weeks since she'd returned from New York, and she still didn't believe that she'd not only run into Avery but also established a tenuous flirtation. True, it was long-distance flirtation and mostly in the form of texts, but Avery had yet to lose interest, allowing Winter's sustained hope that, at some point, they'd segue into more advanced forms of communication. In her daydreamier moments, she even let herself believe there'd be a real date and actual kissing in their future. But for now, she savored their burgeoning connection.

Their last communication had ended abruptly—just when it was getting good—and an unnerving span of time had passed since then. Worried that she'd somehow driven Avery away,

Winter reviewed the conversation in her mind. She'd shared perhaps too much detail about her upcoming work trip to Iowa when Avery rescued them from the mundane.

Do you ever travel for fun?

That depends. What did you have in mind?

They'd danced around the idea of spending a long weekend together in New York, but before any real plans had been made, Avery cut the conversation short.

And now, rather than picking up where they'd left off, Winter found herself spectating a tepid debate over acceptable float adornment taking place at the front of the high school gymnasium. There, beneath the banner proclaiming they were in the "Home of the Fighting Hammers," Martin Cavanaugh bickered about tissue paper flowers and float skirt length with Irene Trout, whose surname befit her perpetually downturned mouth. Martin's salt-and-pepper bowl cut swayed mesmerizingly with his gesticulations. Even in the face of such a visually stunning tableau, Winter found it nearly impossible to feign interest and stole a glance at her still-dormant phone.

"I saw that," Gabe whispered, his handsome face entirely too close for comfort.

"Shh. I'm trying to focus." She didn't dare make eye contact.

Gabe pointedly sniffed the air around her. "Do you smell that? I think your pants are on fire."

A stern glance from Connie Hines, the Beautification committee president, did little to dissuade Gabe and his quest for information.

"When the queen of proper meeting decorum and most vocal member of the anti-phone brigade can't stop checking her phone, there's something going on, and I demand to know what."

"Absolutely nothing is going on," she hissed, hoping, but doubting, he'd drop it.

"Maybe I can help with that."

He promptly took out his own phone, pulled up a picture, and—giving her no choice in the matter—thrust it in her direction. There on display was yet another of Gabe's matchmaking efforts—their numbers were legion. This one apparently had a love-hate relationship with humidity, as evidenced by the dirty-blond frizz that framed her plain but not unattractive face.

"What am I looking at?" Winter asked as quietly as possible.

"Justine. She's pretty, right?"

"She's lovely. Can we pay attention to the meeting now?"

"This is more important."

"More important than finalizing the St. Patrick's Day parade route? I don't think so."

"It's the same route every year. So is the forty minutes of debate to decide that, once again, the parade will start on the south end of Main Street and head north to The Tap. Discussion is a formality that hardly requires our attention."

"But the mayor is looking at us like he wants to give us detention."

"That's the problem with having a part-time mayor whose day job is high school principal."

"Still, I don't want my first detention to come a decade and a half after graduation."

"You just want to avoid this conversation." His whisper decreased ever so slightly in volume, but his sass increased to compensate.

"Has it occurred to you that maybe there's a reason for that?"

"What reason? Avery?"

A pointed throat clearing from the front of the gymnasium silenced Winter's retort. She mouthed the word *stop*, doubting it would deter her friend in the slightest.

"You can't ignore a perfectly good opportunity just because you bumped into your high school crush. That story doesn't even have a sexy ending."

"Not yet anyway." She surprised herself by saying that, and judging by his wide-eyed expression, she'd surprised Gabe too. "For your information, we've been texting." She smiled at the memory of their last exchange.

"You got me all excited over texting? It's obviously been too long since you've had sex or you'd know that this"—he gestured dismissively at her phone—"is a poor substitute."

"For your information, I appreciate getting to know someone before getting into bed with them."

"And for your information, texting does not a relationship make. You and Avery aren't betrothed. You're not even really dating. Meanwhile, Justine is available, interested, and in the same time zone."

"If you two are finished chatting about Winter's sex life, it's time to take a vote." Martha Tennant, town librarian and the human embodiment of prim and proper, peered at them over the top of her glasses.

"Yes, ma'am," they said in unison.

"But for the record, Gabriel has a point."

A chorus of agreement rose up from the remainder of the assemblage.

"This could not get more embarrassing." Winter buried her head in her hands, desperately hoping that she was right.

CHAPTER EIGHT

The remainder of the meeting unfolded more or less routinely, with the mayor's standard grousing about budgets and the subsequent rebuttal from stalwart bookkeeper Phyllis Finch. Ultimately, they added three events to the calendar, tabled the discussion of a town bat house building event as a possible way to celebrate International Bat Appreciation Day, and once again foisted the responsibility for Pride planning on Winter and Gabe, the only queers involved in the special events committee. It meant even more responsibility for both of them, but the workload was preferable to a Pride celebration planned by resident gorgon Marilyn Hines or any of the other well-intentioned but misguided members of the committee. Thankfully, they avoided further discussion of Winter's sex life, but the possibility of it resurfacing hung over her head like the sword of Damocles.

As was their habit after the tumult of town meetings, she and Gabe headed to The Anneville Tap to catch Noah up on all of the town happenings and any new events taking place at the bar.

Since joining the special events committee, Gabe had made it his mission to incorporate his husband's business in every town event. Thus far he'd found a bar angle for at least sixty percent of the town's social calendar.

She fully expected Gabe to use their walk to the bar as an opportunity to resume his pursuit of a happy pairing between Winter and the latest mate of his choice, but he avoided the topic entirely. Instead, he chattered excitedly about his grandiose ideas for Anneville Pride—a monumental celebration, indeed, if she failed to curtail his tendency toward excess. Had it been anyone else, she might have believed he'd taken the hint, but for the past decade, Gabe had made it his mission to pair her off with any willing woman-loving woman he could find. If it wasn't so much effort to extricate herself from his misguided attempts, it would be sweet. And even though she suspected his silence on the matter was merely a pause, she appreciated the reprieve from the reminder that she was on track to be a spinster.

She half listened as he fired off ideas, the lightning pace of his delivery transforming his words into an auditory blur. Instead of working to keep up with plans that would undoubtedly shift and change in the coming weeks, she allowed her thoughts to turn to the topic they'd explored most often lately—Avery. They'd crammed a month's worth of conversation into just a couple of weeks, and in that time, she'd endeavored to learn everything she could about Avery.

So far, she'd heard all about Avery's career and the pop diva who tormented her regularly. To Winter, it seemed an unfair exchange—all the effort and headache of managing a personality just for a paycheck. In fairness, she had no idea how much a music producer earned, but considering the humorous anecdotes Avery had shared about galas and award shows and the perils of the red carpet, it was probably a considerable amount. Thankfully, none of the stories had cameo appearances by girlfriends or lovers. Not that she thought Avery had led a life of celibacy, but Winter had thus far successfully avoided all thoughts of her sexual past, preferring to focus on their hopeful future.

"Someone's distracted." Gabe's voice snapped her out of her thoughts, as he grabbed her arm to steer her into the bar she almost strolled right past.

"Thanks for bringing me back." She wouldn't have minded more time spent dwelling on Avery, but the sooner they caught Noah up on the latest gossip-laden goings-on of the events committee, the sooner she could reach out to the person she really wanted to talk to.

She took a seat at the bar and braced herself for the synchronized shenanigans of her romantically enterprising friends, but even then, Gabe remained focused on the actual matter at hand. Rather than instantly recruiting Noah to pester Winter about her questionable life choices, he merely sipped his Dirty Banana and launched into a strictly business speech to a thoroughly enraptured Noah.

"Did the mayor have to separate you two again?" he asked, a puckish grin sliding into place.

"That was one time," Gabe answered defensively.

"If you could stay focused, it would be no times," she reminded him.

"If they could be more interesting, I'd have a better chance of staying focused." He shrugged as if to suggest it wasn't his fault that he had the attention span of a Goldfish cracker.

As Gabe continued his lightning-speed recap of the productive hour they'd just spent, paying special attention to any impending business for The Tap, Winter referred to her notes to check his accuracy. With only a handful of fanciful departures from the bland, boring truth, he recounted the meeting in less than half the time it had actually taken. More impressive, he never once mentioned Winter's romantic failings or any planned interference. She started to believe she might be in the clear.

"I volunteered the bar to host the Easter egg coloring contest."

"You do know that's for kids, right?" Noah pointed out the obvious flaw in Gabe's plan.

"Kids come with parents, don't they? And if I had to deal with egg-obsessed gremlins on a massive sugar high, I know I'd want a cocktail to take the edge off."

"He has a point," Winter said.

"Thank you." He bestowed an appreciative smile on her. "We'll also have to come up with some themed cocktails for Earth Day. The post-clean-up refreshments are here, and then we have Momosas for Mother's Day."

"Do all events lead to my bar?"

"We're still trying to find a bar angle for Ride Like the Wind Day. Some overly cautious naysayers worry about mixing alcohol and cycling."

"It's a kids' bike-a-thon," Winter pointed out.

"Am I the only one who thinks about the adults in these scenarios?"

"I love that you've made it your mission to help my bottom line."

"Well, I'm a big fan of your bottom line." Gabe winked.

"You guys are disgustingly cute."

"You could be this cute, too," Gabe said. "If you let us set you up."

"Nice try." She shook her head at her friend's persistence as well as her own naïve belief that she'd escaped it.

"For the record, Noah, you're not included for the half-marathon."

After more than a year of tireless campaigning by the surprisingly sizeable running community in town, Anneville would be hosting its first organized race in the spring. Winter hoped it wouldn't be the last. The planning had been an arduous undertaking—made slightly less so by the experts they'd consulted—and she'd learned so much along the way. She wanted to put her new skillset to use again—not in a running capacity but as an organizer. Plus, community interest was stunningly high, and several runners from other cities and states were participating. Offering a charity angle helped build interest, no doubt, and she looked forward to more opportunities to help the community as well as their favorite causes.

"Doesn't the race pass the bar? Twice?" Gabe huffed.

"It does, but it would be a mistake to route the runners directly into the bar."

"Why don't we just hope that people stop by after?" Noah suggested.

"Fine. For now."

"I'm disappointed that I'll miss the race. I really want to know how it all turns out."

"What do you mean you're missing the race? This is the first I'm hearing of it." Gabe seemed equal parts incensed and intrigued.

"I'll be out of town."

"Why?" they asked in unison.

"For work. You two are being weird."

They shared a look that unnerved Winter. She got the sinking feeling that she was about to have good reason to be cranky with her friends.

"What's going on?"

"Sweetie, you know we love you," Gabe started.

"That's ominous."

"We only want what's best for you," Noah chimed in.

"And you know what that is?" she challenged.

"No, but I doubt that it's putting your life on hold to text with your high school fantasy."

Gabe's words stung, but she didn't refute them.

"You're more likely to find your someone closer to home, and we're happy to help."

She tuned him out, more or less successfully. She didn't want to argue—what would be the point?—so she let him talk, but she refused to believe he was right. Love was supposed to be magical, not convenient or practical.

"If I text Justine right now, she'd be here in under fifteen minutes." Gabe held up his phone in an almost threatening way.

"No need, love." Noah kissed him on the temple. "I reached out an hour ago. She's already sitting at a cozy table in the back corner of the bar."

"Should I read anything into the softer than usual lighting?"

"Maybe I'm trying to conserve energy."

"In one corner of the bar?"

Noah shrugged almost playfully.

"You are so good at this." Gabe bestowed an adoring gaze on his partner in meddling.

"Not the words I would use," Winter muttered and pointedly ignored the murky corner in question.

She had no interest in Justine and hated the idea of engaging in a pointless mating ritual just to satisfy her friends. For that matter, she questioned Justine's interest in being a pawn in the boys' scheme. Even if she'd happily agreed to meet a friend of theirs, that decision couldn't have been made unless she'd been left in the dark regarding Winter's unwilling participation. No matter what Gabe said, she saw a possible future with Avery and wanted to see where things went, a curiosity that precluded potential romantic entanglements with perfectly fine strangers.

"I also sent her a pomegranate martini from you. No charge." Noah winked at Winter and smiled, as if he expected some kind of reward or gratitude for making this situation so much more complicated than necessary.

"That's my cue to leave." She rose from her seat only to immediately change course when she locked eyes with Justine, who smiled and raised her valentine-red drink in salute. "She thinks I'm going to join her."

"She doesn't have to be wrong."

"Yes, she does. Even if I wasn't already in a relationship—"

"A what now?" Gabe asked, his eyebrow arched imperiously.

"Fine. The prelude to a relationship. Which means I'm not interested in meeting, flirting with, or dating anyone else. But if I was interested, I could find my own date."

"History suggests otherwise."

"So I'm hopeless when it comes to dating. Does that mean we should stop taking other people's feelings into consideration? Because now, I either have to leave without acknowledging Justine, which would be rude, or I have to go have an awkward conversation with her about well-meaning friends and how impossible they are."

"Or you could have a warm, wonderful, soul-stirring conversation with someone who's not a daydream and then have a very fun night, if you know what I mean." He wiggled his eyebrows suggestively.

"As usual, the whole world knows what you mean."

"Then I must be right."

"I'm pretty sure that's not how quarrels work."

"Then prove me wrong. Go talk to her."

"Okay, I will," she agreed, more out of a desire to shut Gabe up than an actual interest in a conversation—soul-stirring or otherwise—with anyone other than Avery. "But if this doesn't work, you forfeit all future interference in my love life."

"And if I don't?" asked a likely undeterred Gabe.

"Then you're uninvited to Christmas."

Noah gasped at the threat—Winter's holiday celebrations put most other fêtes to shame, so missing one was absolutely not an option—but Gabe merely nodded in agreement. As she approached the newly intimate corner of the bar, he called after her, "If this doesn't work, I'll start looking for cats to keep you warm at night."

Her shoulders dropped in defeat—no doubt Gabe would follow through on that promise—but she plastered on her friendliest smile and stepped up to Justine's table, prepared to make the best of a less-than-ideal situation. After brief and minimally awkward introductions during which Justine nervously folded, unfolded, and refolded her cocktail napkin, Winter opted to fast-forward to the hopefully gentle letdown, sort of like ripping off the courtship bandage.

"I'm so sorry about this, but—"

"You're not single, are you?"

"Not entirely." She scrunched her face apologetically.

Justine's posture relaxed immediately. "That's a relief." At Winter's surprised expression, she immediately backpedaled. "Not that you aren't prime dating material. Really, you're gorgeous, and I would not be upset in any way to go out with you. I mean, who would? It's just that I'm new to town, and I'm still getting my bearings. Plus, you're basically the queen of

Anneville, so we'd be starting off on uneven footing, and that's never good for a relationship."

"Maybe we can settle for a friendship," Winter suggested. "I'd be happy to show you around sometime. In a completely platonic way."

"I may take you up on that."

"I'm curious, though, why did you agree to meet me?" She wondered if Justine had been subject to the same harassment she had.

"When Noah said he wanted to set me up with a friend of his, I was hoping he meant Daphne."

"The bartender?"

"I saw her the first time I came here, for the Bloody Mary Blood Drive last month. I've been coming in a lot since then. We've talked a few times, but I haven't had the nerve to ask her out."

"Why don't you invite her to join you for a drink?"

"Do you really think I should?"

"Absolutely. You're here, you look fantastic—why not take advantage of the situation?" Justine still hesitated, her face a nervous rictus. "I can ask her for you if you'd like."

"No. I'll do it." She rose and marched over to the bar, freeing Winter from any further obligations.

"Noah, you're going to have to cover the bar for a while," she said. As Winter gathered her things, Daphne mixed a pair of drinks and then abandoned her post behind the bar. "I'm going to go home and talk to my non-girlfriend."

CHAPTER NINE

Winter should have sent Avery a text and then started packing for her impending work trip—three cities in two different states taking up just under two weeks of her time. That was the sensible thing to do. Which was probably why she dialed Avery's number and listened to each ring with a nervous excitement she hadn't felt in years, possibly since the first time she fell for Avery.

"This is a nice surprise." When Avery answered, her voice sent a little thrill through Winter's body. "I hope you're calling to tell me you're standing in my lobby right now, waiting for me to invite you up."

"That would be kind of challenging since I don't know where you live."

"We need to change that. Hop on a plane, and I promise to make it worth the trip."

"I'm supposed to head in the opposite direction tomorrow for work."

"Can I convince you to call in sick? I promise to make you soup."

"You make soup?"

"I'm not a savage. I have a microwave and perfectly good can opener."

Winter laughed, delighting in their easy give-and-take. She genuinely enjoyed their exchanges. Avery's confidence and charm were a potent combination, and every time they chatted, Winter fell just a little further under her spell.

"The promise of canned soup notwithstanding, I can't call in sick."

"Have you tried?" The intimacy of her voice in Winter's ear was almost irresistible.

"Once, three years ago, and Peter almost quit on me. I'm the boss."

"So who are you going to get in trouble with?"

"My clients. And Peter. He'll be furious about spending time in Wyoming if I'm not there for him to taunt."

"I can't believe you're picking time in Wyoming with a saucy employee over me."

"I kind of can't believe it either."

There was a brief pause in the conversation, which Winter spent marveling at the stroke of luck that brought Avery back into her life.

"My friends tried to set me up on a blind date tonight," she blurted.

"Oh really?"

"They're kind of obsessed with finding me a girlfriend, and they have zero respect for boundaries."

"Do you want them to respect boundaries? I don't know if that's okay for me to ask. I'm trying to play it cool, but I also really hope you declined the date."

"I actually ended up setting my would-be date up with someone else."

"That was generous of you."

"You're not jealous, are you?"

"I kind of am," Avery admitted, much to Winter's surprise. "If not for a thousand or so miles between us, we'd be having this conversation in person, though not this exact conversation because it would be a bit rude of your friends to set you up with someone when you were already on a date."

"And what would we do on this date?"

"We wouldn't talk about other women, for one thing."

"I'm not interested in Justine. Or anyone else," she said, hoping her declaration was mutual.

"I'm happy to hear that. Now, if I could just convince you to change your travel plans…"

"Keep talking."

"Really?" Avery's surprise was evident.

"Probably not. I just like to hear your voice."

The conversation continued for almost another hour, with Avery taking full advantage of her newfound power. On top of regaling her with humorous stories from work, Avery renewed her campaign for a drastic change in Winter's travel plans. Her persistence was admirable, and by the end of the call, she had Winter seriously reconsidering that spontaneous trip to New York.

The next morning, Winter set off on her business trip feeling tired but overly optimistic, even for her. She'd stayed up far too late talking to Avery—a conversation that had reaffirmed her conviction that a future with Avery sat closer to reality than Gabe was willing to admit. Contrary to his assertion that she was more likely to find romance closer to home, she refused to believe that love should be convenient rather than magical, and her connection to Avery, despite the miles between them, proved it.

Unfortunately, she soon realized that the propitious launch of her trip would be its high point. She endured flight delays and cancellations, which at first didn't faze her. The likelihood of transportation snafus was why she built in extra time for travel. What she hadn't planned for was the airline losing her luggage. On all her trips, she'd always ended up in the same place as her belongings. As she watched the same three bags that weren't hers and a box labeled *Human Tissue*—which probably should have been retrieved by that point—repeatedly circle the Jackson Hole Airport baggage carousel, she realized she'd taken clean underpants for granted.

Fortunately, most of her supplies had made the trip safely, and Peter filled in several of the important gaps, but the situation made for a more stressful job than necessary. Though she and her assistant improvised easily when the need arose, she felt off-kilter the entire time, like she wasn't quite reaching her normally high standards. Her client, however, didn't seem to notice that anything was amiss. She spent the majority of the ten-hour shoot strutting around the set, complimenting everything she saw, her corduroy pants providing a mesmerizing soundtrack in her wake.

The upside to the calamity of her day was that she had something to share with Avery during their nightly chat. She was sweet and sympathetic—more evidence that Winter wasn't wasting her time, no matter what Gabe had to say about it—wishing her a better day tomorrow. Sadly, the deity in charge of workplace wish fulfillment opted to ignore that request, and the downward spiral of Winter's work trip continued.

The photographer for the next shoot showed up late, inebriated, and essentially useless, wasting everyone's time, throwing Winter's carefully constructed schedule out of whack and amplifying her appreciation for Macy's professionalism. Though the make-up day was largely uneventful thanks, she suspected, to the photographer's massive hangover, she would have preferred to spend what should have been downtime prepping for the next job as her now faulty itinerary dictated. Still, she was a professional, and she would make the best of the situation.

As she microwaved tampons to create picture-perfect steam for the broccoli cheddar soup awaiting its moment in the spotlight, she fiddled with her phone. She didn't have time to start a conversation with Avery, but that didn't mean she couldn't review the highlights of their recent conversations.

"Looks like those tampons aren't the only thing getting steamy." Peter's voice in her ear startled her. "Macy and I have been dying for a salacious update on your city sweetheart. Spill all the details."

On the last job before she returned home and hopefully reunited with her luggage, she allowed her mind to wander a bit too freely on thoughts of her house and her bed and her plenitude of frequent flier miles. More than enough for a trip to New York. She'd woken up to a good-morning text, suggesting that she reward herself for her hard work with a little vacation to the city, and she'd been considering it ever since. She even kept her phone out on the counter where she could easily glance at it throughout the day. While she should have been focused on the heat gun she held and the chocolate ganache she was adding a glossy sheen to, she found herself lost in thought about Avery and seeing her in person. Distracted, she overheated the chocolate, liquefying it and sending it oozing across the counter toward her phone. Reflexively, she turned the heat away from the seeping chocolate mess and directly onto her phone. She'd never seen a melted cell phone before. The situation went from bad to worse when the chocolate made its way to what used to be her phone, coating the mess that had been her lifeline to Avery.

"Well," Peter said, "this might be the one instance when chocolate doesn't make everything better."

CHAPTER TEN

By the time she returned from her calamitous business trip, she had a replacement phone—with none of her contacts from the melted one—and a strong desire to wash the bad luck of the past two weeks away before getting a good night's sleep. Sadly, her hot water heater refused to cooperate. No matter how long she let the water run, the temperature never rose above nippy, and the thought of a cryogenic shower on an already chilly night was almost enough to darken her sunny disposition. At that hour, she knew a call to Anneville's resident plumber would go unanswered, but she would put him on the case first thing in the morning. Three days and fifteen hundred dollars later, hot water flowed from her taps like her pipes ran directly to the earth's molten core, but her hope for a banner year had dimmed.

On a more positive note, Miss Opal, the octogenarian who owned the other half of Winter's duplex, shared her fully functioning plumbing until Winter could bathe without the risk of hypothermia. That the gift of a hot shower came with great conversation was a benefit she couldn't overlook. And if not for the inconvenience of her hot water heater's demise, Winter might have missed the opportunity to catch up with Miss Opal and the latest news of the town over coffee in her neighbor's spotless kitchen, a treat she'd been too busy to indulge in recently. So, in a way, the whole mess was really something of a blessing.

"You missed Chief Dwyer's latest brush with disaster." Miss Opal chuckled as she refilled their coffee mugs.

"What happened this time?"

"He locked himself in the back of his police car."

"Again?"

"Beverly needs to set up a tent on their lawn or stop kicking him out."

"Did she at least have a good reason this time?"

Miss Opal shook her head. "He gave her nephew a speeding ticket."

As Miss Opal launched into the humorous tale of the poor chief of police facing punishment from his wife for enforcing the law, Winter allowed herself to appreciate not just the story but also the utter peculiarity of her hometown. Apparently, rather than spending the night in a hotel or on a friend's couch, the chief opted to sleep in his cruiser, forgetting that the rear doors don't open from the inside. He had to ask his wife to let him out, which she did, but only after a crowd gathered to witness the event.

"I hope she let him back in the house after that."

"He still had to apologize to the nephew and pay the ticket himself."

In the comfortable silence that followed the tale of Stanley Dwyer's latest gaffe, Winter wondered if Miss Opal, queen of gossip and living library of Anneville's residents old and new, would be a good source of information on Avery. She doubted that her neighbor would have Avery's contact information, but there were other ways she might be helpful.

"What do you know about the Sumners?" she asked innocently.

"Why are you interested in old Grumpy and Sourpuss?"

"No particular reason." She felt the heat of a blush on her cheeks and avoided eye contact.

"That must be why you can't look me in the eye. Want to try that again?"

"I'm sort of pre-dating their daughter," she said before offering the abridged version of her stalled romance with Avery. "I was hoping they might give me her number since I lost it." She dropped her romantically useless phone on the table.

"They'd be as likely to have Beyoncé's number. They stopped talking to their daughter years ago."

Though she appreciated the obscure insight into Avery's aversion to Anneville, Winter couldn't fathom being so isolated from her family when they were alive, and her heart broke a little for Avery.

"Now, I never got the full story," Miss Opal continued, "but I think that it had something to do with the aunt."

So much for their help, she thought, her disappointment growing. She wanted to ask what had happened between the Sumners and their daughter to cause such a rift, but she also wanted to respect Avery's privacy. If she wanted Winter to know the details, she could share them herself, assuming they ever connected again.

She thanked Miss Opal for her hospitality and rose to leave. "I have to start shopping for the Eggstravaganza. I've taken charge of the bulk of the planning this year."

"Don't you ever do things just for yourself?"

"I like helping other people, so this is doing something for myself."

Miss Opal smiled and shook her head. "This town doesn't deserve you."

That afternoon, after a prolonged grocery store excursion, she had ample supplies and a plan for her festive masterpiece. What she didn't have was time or energy to begin the involved task of creating her extravagant Easter offerings. So, as the afternoon sun began its slow descent, she decided to take the long way home, the way that would take her past The Tap and the possibility of friendly conversation, assuming the bar wasn't too busy.

She didn't even get a chance to assess the situation before Gabe grabbed her by the arm and dragged her inside. "Thank god you're here. You're the answer to our party prayers."

Noah stood behind the bar, waging war on a defenseless bowl of strawberries. She set her bags down, draped her coat over a barstool, and moved behind the bar.

"What did these poor strawberries ever do to you?" She scooted him aside to relieve him of his butchering.

"They refused to work with me."

"I can't say I blame them."

He handed over his paring knife, and in just a few minutes, she'd deftly fanned several berries and cut others into hearts and roses while Noah played to his strengths and mixed cocktails for the three of them. As soon as it was presented to him, Gabe took a dramatic sip of his drink and sighed heavily.

"Why did I ever offer to host the Welcome to Spring Spectacular? It's grueling to be a top-tier host."

"You must be exhausted from watching other people work," Winter teased as she continued turning berries into fantastic shapes.

"Delegating is just as important as doing."

"More so if you have no applicable skills."

"Someone's feeling haughty this afternoon." Gabe produced a whole watermelon that she eyed warily. "Do tell. Is there a salacious cause for this newfound superciliousness? And does it come in the form of a special lady?"

"Not likely," she said before she had time to consider the consequences. Knowing she had no way out of their interrogation, she shared the latest obstacle on her path to romantic bliss with Avery. "What if I never hear from her again?"

"In that case, I'd be happy to help you out, but I've been forbidden from offering my assistance." He popped a butterfly-shaped strawberry in his mouth and offered an expression that was half pout, half gloat.

"Have you tried Googling her?" Noah asked.

"I don't want to Internet stalk my theoretical girlfriend."

"Not even if you could get her phone number out of it?" Gabe whipped his phone out, prepared for the hunt.

"How? It's not the yellow pages."

"She does work, doesn't she? How do her clients find her?"

That was actually a good point, one she wished she had thought of before recruiting the boys' help. "Okay. You can look her up a little. But just for a phone number."

"Right, right. Of course," he said, already engrossed in his search. He gasped not a minute later. "Oh my."

"What? What is it?"

"Did you know she dated a supermodel?"

"How is that helpful? You're supposed to be looking for a phone number."

"This is more interesting." She scowled at him as he continued scrolling. "I didn't see a professional page for her, but oh, is there gossip."

"I don't want to hear it." On that point, she was resolute. She had no interest in sensational headlines or gossip that might affect her view of Avery.

"You are no fun."

"Shut up and hand me that watermelon."

At home later that night, she made herself a cup of tea, considered getting a start on her Easter preparations, but instead ended up staring at her new phone with all its fancy features, none of which happened to be Avery's contact information. If only her mildly obsessive behavior had included memorizing Avery's phone number. For a moment, she considered picking up the Internet search where Gabe had left off. He hadn't really stayed on topic anyway. But, she thought as her finger hovered over the Chrome icon on her smartphone, Gabe said he hadn't found a way to contact her. What made her think she could succeed where he'd failed? The man practically lived on his phone. And she'd already invaded Avery's privacy enough for one day. She didn't want to risk the temptation of all the Internet had to offer. Her only option, it seemed, was hoping and waiting for Avery to contact her.

It took almost another week of worry before Winter heard from Avery. As each day passed without any communication, her concern mounted, and her quest for distractions increased in direct proportion to the degree of sadness she was trying to hide from. Which is how she ended up convincing the owners of Poke Nom, the surprisingly popular niche restaurant in downtown Anneville, to not only expand their advertising campaign but also let her style their wares for said ads. They certainly didn't need her help to attract diners, but she was more than happy to spend a day styling bowls of raw fish rather than trying to will Avery to call her.

She also updated her website, started her spring cleaning, and volunteered to take over the baking duties for Margie Schnitz's birthday party. That undertaking quickly morphed from a simple cake to a three-tiered masterpiece that no one at the party felt qualified to cut, plus an elaborate array of cupcakes in various flavors, all elaborately decorated. Those in attendance were doubly glad to see Winter's contribution—not only was it remarkable, but it also spared them from the dessert offerings of Margie's mother, whose kitchen debacles were legendary.

Winter also devoted an inordinate amount of time to perfecting her Easter contributions, which explained why it was even more over the top this year. Did the town need giant chocolate eggs or edible handwoven Easter baskets? Of course not. But her fellow Annevillians would appreciate her efforts, and that carried its own kind of reward. That the pursuit of the perfect egg-to-basket ratio kept her mind mostly off the unplanned hiatus in her love life was just an added bonus.

She was so intently focused on her handiwork that she almost didn't answer the phone when it rang. Not only was she doing battle with her latest practice egg, but she'd also run out of polite ways to reject scammers and telemarketers alike. She didn't think she could handle another disappointment. On the other hand, she had nothing to lose but a few minutes of her time, a commodity she was avidly trying to discard. The second she heard Avery's voice, she celebrated the unflagging hopefulness that had finally paid off.

"I'm so glad you called," she said.

"I'm so glad you answered. You had me a little worried since I hadn't heard from you in a while."

"I'm so sorry about that," she said before explaining in a rush why she hadn't been in contact lately.

And just like that, they fell into an easy back-and-forth, their banter flowing as if there hadn't been an unfortunate lapse in their communication. As they talked, Winter abandoned her work, moved to her living room, and got comfortable on the couch where she could better appreciate this time with Avery. She repeatedly tried to get Winter to visit, despite the limitations of her travel-heavy schedule.

"You travel an awful lot for your job. Maybe you should move closer to where the work is."

"My work takes me all over the country, so where would that be?"

"How about anywhere but Anneville? There can't be much work for you there."

"You know, planes fly in this direction. You could always come see me."

"And what would we do in Anneville?"

The question hung in the air, laced with meaning. Winter suspected it was more a commentary on the mundanity of small-town living, but she didn't have to let the slight against her hometown stand.

"I have a few ideas," she answered in her best kittenish purr.

"Now I need to know what you're thinking."

"Come see me and find out." If they were having this conversation in person, Winter surely would have blown the seductress act by winking or blushing or, more likely, both. Suddenly she was grateful for the miles that separated them.

"Tempting," Avery said, and Winter thought for a moment that she'd soon have a visitor. But then Avery segued to a different topic, and though she was a little disappointed not to get a clear answer, she was mostly elated to keep the conversation going. They covered topics from family, with Avery carefully skirting any definitive commentary on hers, to their adolescence, to still more attempts to schedule a visit. By the end of their call, they'd managed to plan an in-person date. They'd have to wait a few more weeks before their schedules cooperated, but she knew the wait would be worth it.

When they finally hung up, Winter's practice egg had long since solidified into an amorphous confectionary blob that not even the most hard-core chocolate lover would find appealing. All her work that evening had been for nothing, but she didn't care. She and Avery were finally back on track, and she made sure to write down her contact information in three separate locations, just to be safe.

CHAPTER ELEVEN

What a difference a phone call made. Winter had gone from trying to bake away her stress and anxiety to being impossibly buoyant in the span of one conversation. And she didn't even care of it was too much, too soon, she planned to talk to Avery again that night. She already knew where this was heading—Gabe's opinion of the matter notwithstanding, they were kind of already dating, just without all the kissing or any physical contact. But that would change soon enough, and until then, she intended to get her Avery fix from frequent conversations. If only she could make the time until their first official date pass faster—even her patience had its limits.

In the meantime, she was singing in her shower and in her car and even a little in the security line at the airport. A bit of side-eye from a TSA agent brought that to an abrupt end, but by the time she met up with Peter in the Philadelphia airport, she'd started singing another verse of "Walking on Sunshine," much to his chagrin.

"You're way too happy, even for you," he grumbled as they moved through the crowds of travelers, several of whom seemed to share his disdain for the first half of the day.

"Maybe I have good reason to be happy," she teased but tamed her inner songstress all the same.

"Good reason for you to be happy, or for regular people? Because you become euphoric over clean sheets, so either you recently hit the jackpot at a linens sale, or—" Without warning, he stopped, causing a small pileup behind him. "You've been a naughty girl, haven't you? I'm so proud of you."

"A phone call hardly qualifies as naughty." She started walking toward the baggage claim again, a newly energized Peter in tow.

"Depends on what you talk about."

"We talked a lot about work and family." Only her family, and she again considered Avery's deflection as she reflected on the conversation. She'd have to correct that the next time they spoke.

"I was hoping for something more in the 'What are you wearing?' genre."

"That didn't come up."

His lips puckered into a disappointed moue. "I'm going to need more from this relationship. I want romance and saucy details."

"How do you think I feel?"

"There's hope for you yet." He plucked the first of their bags from the carousel. "I expect an update when you have something salacious to report."

"That's not going to happen." She added another bag to their collection. "You do remember I'm your boss, don't you?"

"And I'm working really hard right now."

In spite of the compounded joy of her promising relationship status and being in the same time zone as Avery for a challenging-in-a-good-way job, she still felt a twinge of remorse over missing the inaugural Anneville Half-marathon. She'd tried to reschedule for after the race, but the client, Gordon Cutler, was insistent. He also claimed to have connections to *Simmer Down*, a publication she'd wanted to work with for years, so in order to maintain her impeccable reputation and get in good with Gordon, she agreed to his terms. An opportunity like this was simply too important. She couldn't bring herself to say no. Nor could she change the date of the race, so here she was, missing an event she'd been so excited about. At least Gabe would send her updates.

On that note, he really should have shared something by now. The race hadn't started yet, but volunteers and organizers should have been putting the final touches on everything. She was sure he hadn't forgotten. Mostly sure, anyway.

"One little reminder won't hurt," she told herself before firing off the tiniest of texts to check in.

How's the race prep going?

You're dead to me.

Winter didn't know what she'd done, but she expected an explanation forthwith.

I've been working on your race since four this morning, which means I've been awake since three. On a SATURDAY. Weekends are for sleeping.

I asked Beulah to order coffee for the race crew.

This level of tired requires more coffee than the Western Hemisphere can hold.

She offered her most sincere apologies for his suffering. Then, because she had to know, she repeated her question.

Does this mean you're too tired to make sure the race goes off without a hitch?

Shouldn't you be playing with potatoes or stuffing a turkey or something?

Close. I'm dealing with desserts.

Whatever. I'm sure it requires more of your attention than this meticulously planned and certain to run smoothly race you abandoned. Stop worrying and go make pretty.

Almost immediately, she received a photo of a bleary-eyed Gabe standing in front of an impressive pack of runners at the starting line. Aside from her friend, everything appeared to be in order, and even with his half-closed eyes and pout, he looked mildly pleased with himself.

Maybe you'll be awake for the next update, she teased.

I hope you melt another phone. Really, Gabe was exceptionally grumpy when he was tired.

I love you, too, she answered, hoping that he'd feel better once the sun rose.

Reassured that the race was in good hands, she turned her focus back to the task at hand—desserts and sweets of every kind, all waiting for their moment in the spotlight. She and Peter fell into an easy rhythm honed over the many jobs they'd completed together. They collaborated wordlessly, creating gorgeous displays of delectable-looking desserts. While he tamed some uncooperative strawberries for a shortcake in need of a topping, she carefully placed crumbs around the array of cookies that Gordon wanted to feature.

The local but rapidly growing bakery they were styling for was expanding into a wider market and using Winter's expertise to entice customers. If all went well with this round of ads, she might be looking at a national campaign.

Several hours passed before she reluctantly took a break at Gordon's insistence. While Peter stepped outside for a dose of sunshine and the inhabitants of video village conferred about the progress and the plan for the rest of the day, she hunted down flights to New York. Her trip to Avery was still six weeks away, but preparation was her friend. She booked a flight and made a backup plan in case of a travel emergency. Although the trip planning was in its extremely early stages, she couldn't help but share her progress with Avery. So, she sent a screenshot of her flight confirmation and added a note that she'd see her in six weeks.

Finding a hotel was her next step—though she imagined that she'd be welcome to stay with Avery, she didn't want to presume too much. Plus, she preferred to have options. She didn't want to rush anything. She'd been waiting decades for this opportunity, and now that it was here, she wanted to savor every moment. Beyond that, she wanted what she hoped was developing between them to do so naturally, not out of convenience or some sort of quid pro quo obligation. And, should the date not go well, she'd have a place to retreat to rather than spending an awkward night with a failed suitor. But, honestly, in this instance, she'd happily pay for a hotel room she never used.

I would have taken care of that for you. Avery's text interrupted the hunt for lodgings.

Now you don't have to.

I'll have to find some other way to tend to your needs.

Can't wait.

She wondered how she was supposed to work with that promise on her mind.

As soon as she sent the text, Gordon approached to discuss his ideas for the pie portion of the day. Winter dutifully tucked her phone safely in her back pocket and focused almost all her attention on Gordon and his specific styling needs.

By the time they wrapped shooting for the day, Winter was covered in so many different sticky liquids that her apron looked like she'd shared kitchen duty with Jackson Pollock. She doubted there was a sauce, cream, meringue, or glaze in the entire state of Pennsylvania that hadn't landed on her at some point during her demanding but ultimately rewarding eleven-hour workday. Gordon was thrilled and already making plans for their next collaboration, and as she cleaned up the substantial evidence of a job well done, she decided that the day had been not just a success but a triumph. And how better to end an already marvelous day than to share her joy with Avery?

Opting for a call, she was disappointed when she got voice mail rather than Avery herself. She left a cheery message before returning to her hotel to pack and, she hoped, tell her sort-of girlfriend good night. She considered checking in with Gabe, who had neglected to update her on the race. She wasn't all that surprised, given his foul mood, and considering his all-consuming exhaustion, she doubted he'd still be awake. As the exertion of her own day caught up with her, her eyelids began to droop. Just before she drifted off to sleep, she decided she could pester him just as easily in the morning and probably get better results.

CHAPTER TWELVE

When she woke the next morning, her phone greeted her with zero notifications, a somewhat disappointing but not entirely unexpected development. Had she fallen asleep thinking of Avery and hoping to hear from her? Of course, but she was also glad that they'd both gotten a good night's sleep, assuming Avery hadn't been out all night doing things Winter would rather not think about. Spurred on by that troublesome dip into negativity, she sent a good-morning text, not only to Avery but also to Gabe, who should have been rejuvenated enough to share details of yesterday's race.

People ran. There was sweat and so many more bodily fluids than I ever knew existed. Runners are a disgusting lot, but they can drink. The bar did well at the after-party.

That's the most important thing. She couldn't help but smile at his skewed priorities.

We should definitely have more races.

Your day must have gotten a lot better if you're volunteering to lose more sleep. Considering his foul mood of yesterday, she was surprised that Gabe hadn't sworn off all extracurricular activities.

No, no, no. You're in charge of the next one. My talents are more suited to spectating. From afar. With a Bloody Mary in my hand.

Of course. Well then, I'm glad it went without a hitch.

Me too. After the accident, everything ran smoothly.

She paused, certain for a moment that she'd misread his message. After rereading it and reviewing all of their exchanges from the previous day, she was no closer to clarity. And while she hoped that Gabe hadn't mentioned it because the accident was inconsequential, she wasn't willing to take that for granted. Nor was she willing to leave this conversation to the ambiguity and easy misinterpretation of texting.

"What happened?" she asked as soon as he answered (which took entirely too long considering the bombshell he'd just dropped). "Was anyone hurt?"

"I think you might be overreacting."

"Or maybe you're underreacting. I'd have a better idea if you'd tell me what happened."

He sighed heavily, and she could practically hear his eye roll. "There was just a minor incident at around mile ten."

"Define 'minor incident.'" She couldn't believe he'd withheld this information or that he was so put out by her concern.

"One of the spectators stepped onto the course to get a picture. For what, I'm not sure. Honestly, no one looked particularly photogenic."

"Less editorializing, please."

"So impatient." He tsked. "She collided with one of the runners, and then it was like human dominoes. At least five people went down."

"Oh my god."

"Somehow they took out some scaffolding for one of the time clocks."

"What?" How was this story getting worse?

"And that fell on a runner who pushed another woman out of the way."

"This is a nightmare."

"The equipment was a little scuffed but still functional, and all but one runner finished the race," he said, as if that nullified the damage.

"What about the one who didn't finish?" She braced herself for whatever answer he was about to give.

"The paramedics said she'd be fine."

"Okay, and no disrespect to the volunteer fire department, but did anyone with actual medical knowledge check her out?"

While she appreciated all the good work that her fellow townspeople did to keep Anneville safe, she questioned their largely untested emergency medicine skills. Beyond that, the best members of AVFD had registered to run the race. The remainder of the crew had only joined for the T-shirts and the annual barbecue. Winter had little faith that the well-meaning bumblers left in charge were up to the task of assessing their own well-being, let alone that of someone with a serious injury.

"As a matter of fact, yes. A doctor at the emergency room had the situation under control. And for the record, she's single and attractive, not that you care."

"I'm more concerned with how good she is at her job."

"High marks all around." Gabe shared his inexpert opinion before divulging, somewhat hesitantly, that the runner, Abby Something-or-other, had a mild concussion, a fractured pelvis, and strong chance of being voted Annevillian of the Year.

"Why didn't you tell me this when it happened?" She honestly wasn't sure he would have mentioned it had she not pressed for information.

"Because the situation was under control, and what could you have done other than worry?"

"I could have visited."

"While you were holed up in the land of the cheesesteak?" He scoffed. "Besides, it's family only, and even if you were allowed, I'm not sure the company of a stressed-out stranger would have been beneficial."

"Well then, I could have—" Okay, so he had a point. She didn't necessarily agree that he should have kept this information to himself, but knowing about it sooner wouldn't have changed the outcome. Now that she did know, however, she could do something. She didn't know what, but she had a whole flight home to think about that.

A voice message from Gabe was waiting for her when she landed: "The Special Events Committee sent a stunning bouquet to our injured runner's hospital room, and assuming she's mobile and interested, she gets a free entry into next year's race. Consider yourself covered."

Maybe he'd reconsidered his casual withholding of important information or, more likely, he knew she'd fret over the situation until she found a way to help. She wouldn't exactly rest easy with this new development, but she admitted it was a relief, especially since she hadn't come up with any brilliant plans to comfort the casualty of Anneville's first organized race.

She appreciated the update and the gesture. She wasn't sure she felt comfortable considering herself covered, but she couldn't think of anything else she might do for their poor, injured runner, unless she wanted her hospital food styled. She doubted that would affect the taste in any meaningful way. So, that was one problem sort of solved, she supposed, but she still hadn't heard from Avery. Now that she didn't have to spread cheer at the hospital or hunt down the perfect "Sorry you were grievously injured at an event I was responsible for. Get well soon" bouquet, she had no obligations other than a debriefing and a late but vital lesson in proper emergency communications with Gabe. She could absolutely spare a few minutes to check in with Avery and learn if her weekend had gone any better than Winter's.

Sitting at the bar two hours later, staring at her wineglass but not actually drinking from it, she checked her phone for the zillionth time that evening. Still nothing from Avery. "She's probably busy," she muttered to her stubbornly dormant phone. Her mind tried to concoct all sorts of activities that might keep a previously attentive suitor preoccupied for close to forty-eight hours, but she shut that down with a forceful shake of her head followed by a lingering sigh.

"You're awfully glum for someone who didn't have to babysit a mostly successful athletic event at an offensively early hour." Gabe, having already finished his beverage, relieved her of her untouched drink.

"I'm just waiting to hear from Avery."

"Does she know that?" He grabbed the phone from her hands and scrolled through their recent exchanges. "My, you girls have been busy."

"Can I have my phone back, please?" She didn't have the will to quarrel with him.

"Only if you promise to use it for good, not obsession."

"What does that mean?" She snatched her phone back and placed it out of his reach.

"It means that you won't get anywhere just staring at your phone. If you want answers, find them." He gestured broadly, like one of the models from *The Price Is Right* showing off a fabulous prize.

"I've tried that. Four texts and two voice mails' worth." She'd done everything short of hiring a sky writer, and she hadn't entirely ruled out that option. Another heavy sigh.

"Stalker much?" Her glower did little to curb his cheek. "Instead of scaring her off, maybe you should perform your own investigation. The Internet is your friend."

"How would the Internet know what's preventing Avery from communicating?"

"She's a semicelebrity with links to actual celebrities. Believe me, if there's something worth knowing, you'll find it if you know how to look."

Did that mean Gabe had found something? Something that Winter didn't want to know?

"Regardless, I'm still not interested in spying on her. Besides, those websites are all gossip."

"Fine, have it your way. Just keep waiting for Avery to call." He took another healthy sip of her wine, which he obviously now considered his own. "Assuming she ever does."

Back at home later that night, Gabe's ominous words weighed on her mind. She didn't want to believe that he was right—about

Avery ghosting her or about the likelihood that she'd find some kind of solace from an Internet search. Surely, Winter hadn't imagined the connection between them. Avery had been just as invested in their conversations and the possibility of spending more time together. That's why Winter had so enthusiastically shared her flight information. In retrospect, perhaps that was a mistake. She couldn't see how, especially since the visit had been Avery's repeated suggestion to begin with. Why would her interest in seeing Winter change so drastically from one day to the next? Winter couldn't explain it.

But TMZ could. Gabe's voice rang in her head, spurred on by the close proximity of her laptop.

"One little peek couldn't hurt," she told herself. After all, she was concerned, so it was more like a web-based wellness check than an invasion of privacy. And she didn't have to dally. She could simply do a quick search, and if nothing germane to Avery's current whereabouts or preoccupations popped up, Winter wouldn't go any further.

Ninety minutes later, she was off in the weeds, none of the several open tabs on her laptop even remotely connected to the information she'd told herself she was going in search of. She hadn't meant to go so far afield, of course, but the first item that popped up—before she'd even finished typing Avery's name—was a story in one of those celebrity-focused, fact-lenient publications about Avery's recent public spat with pop superstar Meadow Lane. If she were to believe the brief but sensational article, Avery's relationship with her starlet hadn't been strictly business. The breakup, therefore, had been at least as personal as it was professional, and the author backed her specious claims with an eye-catching picture of Avery, hands pawing at Meadow's minimally clad chest.

Unlike most of America, Winter knew the context of that photo. Or at least she thought she did. Avery had shared with her the details of the failed meeting with Meadow and her manager—who'd been edited right out of the photograph—and her clearly well-founded fears about the public backlash. Winter had done her best to console her, and that was the last they'd spoken of the incident. Winter had no reason to think anything more of it until now.

Article after article linked Avery and Meadow Lane romantically. They all cited the demise of their romance as the reason their musical collaborations came to an end, and without exception, Avery was always at fault—she was alternately jealous of Meadow's fame or pushing her too hard to capitalize on her rising star. Winter didn't want to believe it, but how could she not? Yes, she knew that sites like these thrived on sensationalism and speculation. But it wasn't like Avery was making any effort to deny the rumors either publicly or in private.

"I'm such a fool." She wiped away the tears that blurred her vision and opened a new tab on her computer. She logged in to her airline account and, with minimal difficulties, navigated to the option to cancel her flight. "If I didn't stand a chance with the small-town high school version of Avery, why would famous, successful, big-city Avery be interested in me? I'm the same girl from Anneville that I've always been, and I always will be."

With one click, she put an end to her travel plans and her hopes for a true connection with Avery.

CHAPTER THIRTEEN

Canceling plans and canceling habits were two entirely different beasts, so the demise of her romantic weekend notwithstanding, Winter still spent entirely too much time focused on her phone and its utter lack of communication from Avery. Each morning when she woke up, she couldn't stop herself from hoping that maybe that would be the day she'd get a text or a call. She'd even welcome smoke signals or a carrier pigeon. She wasn't picky. Invariably, she'd cast a hopeful glance at her phone, only to be met with continued disappointment.

Of course, once she had her phone in hand and her mind already on the topic of Avery, it just made sense to reread all their texts, a bad habit that started as a sort of wistful longing for what could have been but quickly progressed into unrestrained self-flagellation. Before long, Winter had expanded her morning coffee ritual to include questioning so many of the things she shared and wishing that she could take them back. Not that Avery was thinking about her or her uncommonly cheery conversation. The stunning lack of communication between them proved that.

Meanwhile, demand for her attention didn't stop simply because her heart was bruised, which was just as well. Evasion was her friend. So, she took on as many jobs as she could realistically handle, and with each undertaking, she tended to her clients' needs with the same care and attention to detail she'd built her reputation on to date. She didn't necessarily enchant those around her with her vivacity, but at least her professional standards hadn't slipped. Not surprisingly, Peter noticed a shift in her demeanor, and being far more invested in her personal life than was healthy, he easily deduced that she'd hit a pothole on the road to romantic bliss. She managed to dodge his queries about her now-dormant love life by giving her work all the attention normally allotted to friendly banter. Likewise, she continued to meet her obligations to Anneville and her various committees. Her heart wasn't in any of it, but that was hardly Anneville's fault.

She finally had a weekend all to herself to focus on some much-needed housework and holiday decorating. Her home and yard were still festooned with the trappings of Mother's Day, and they were almost a full week into June, for goodness' sake. Her Memorial Day décor hadn't even left the box, and it had been weeks since she'd visited the holiday corner of her attic. That would change today.

Dressed in her comfiest leggings and a well-worn Pussycat Dolls T-shirt from her younger sister's bad-music-obsessed teenage years, she threw her hair in a quick, messy ponytail and prepared to embark upon her holiday housework ritual. She was still deciding what music would best suit Pride month with hints of Father's Day when Gabe and Noah burst through the front door, interrupting the first moment of peace she'd had in weeks.

"What are you doing?" Gabe asked. He took one look at her housekeeping casual ensemble and frowned. "It's like you're not even trying anymore."

"Trying what?" She looked to Noah for some kind of explanation. Meanwhile, Gabe disappeared up the stairs. More than a little curious, she followed him to her bedroom, Noah close behind, where they found him rummaging through her closet.

"Can I help you find something?"

"That cute floral tank top you wore a couple of weeks ago. It will be perfect with these jeans"—he tossed the pants in her direction and continued rooting through her wardrobe—"and these sandals. I'll find the top. You just get yourself cleaned up."

"Will someone please tell me what's going on?" She didn't think she could be more confused if she tried.

"We're worried about you, sweetie." Noah placed a gentle hand on her shoulder. "You were supposed to be at the bar an hour ago to help set up."

"Arts and Crafts." She gasped, comprehension dawning. "I completely forgot. Why didn't you remind me?"

"That's why we're here." Gabe emerged from her closet, quarry in hand. His fashion quest complete, he turned his full attention back to her. "Why aren't you showering?" He pushed her to the bathroom, stopping before his feet crossed the threshold. "You have ten minutes, and then we're leaving."

"What if I don't want to go?"

"Attendance is mandatory," Noah called from down the hall.

"I know I promised to help you with the event."

"After dreaming up the idea and insisting that The Tap host."

"And I'm sorry about flaking on you."

"As you should be."

"He means that we understand." Noah scowled at him.

"I appreciate that, but I don't think I can be in charge of people today."

"No problem," Gabe said, his tone softened.

"We just want you to come out and have fun."

"Really?" This didn't sound like the disorganized duo who normally leaned on her skills for all fêtes big and small.

"Really. We've missed you while you've been retreating from life. There's a world outside of waiting for Avery, and you seem to have forgotten that. So you're going to enjoy yourself today, even if we have to force fun upon you."

"Thanks." She pulled both of them close and squeezed them tight. She still wasn't sure she wanted to go, but she couldn't say no to her friends.

A couple of hours later as she milled about enjoying a rare turn as bystander, she began to suspect that the real draw for the bulk of the crowd had been the array of craft beers on hand rather than any of the arts. Rembrandts they were not. In spite of the astounding lack of skill on display, the crowd seemed to be having a good time. In fact, their subpar offerings contributed to the fun rather than ruining it.

She visited each station, trying to decide which of the art projects was most interesting, both creatively and socially. The still-life painting had drawn a small collection of dad-bodied former high school athletes. They kept their drinks close at hand while they dabbed clumsily at their canvasses, and their collective lack of talent did little to prevent good-natured trash talking.

A cabal of ladies with a distinct PTA vibe occupied the origami corner, chatting and folding, the collection of allegedly finished products looking more like paper that had been crumpled with intention rather than any recognizable form. They laughed and compared terrible origami, their mirth increasing with each colorful wad of paper they displayed. Despite staying on the periphery of the crowd, she actually was enjoying herself. As she hopped from art to art and craft to craft, she found herself smiling more than she had in the past three weeks.

Various supplies and half-finished projects were strewn across tables around the bar, while half the crowd milled about, pint glasses in hand. Winter, too, had indulged in perhaps more than her fair share of the craft beers on tap, but there were so many tasty options. She couldn't possibly sample them all, but she could have one more before switching to water. She turned toward the bar and marched directly into Avery, who had the gall to look even better than Winter remembered. Beside her, a young girl who looked about as happy to be there as an acrophobic visiting the top of the Eiffel Tower looked nervously back and forth between them.

"Winter. What are you doing here?"

"Arts. And crafts. Mostly crafts." She held up her empty glass as proof. "Also, I live here, so I'm not the one who's out of place."

"She's got you there," Avery's young companion chimed in.

"Thank you, young lady." Winter smiled at her unexpected ally.

"Does everybody have to gang up on me?"

"Why don't I help with that?" Gabe appeared at Winter's side. "You look like you're old enough for a lesson in proper muddling."

They chatted amicably as they walked away, the girl asking, "Aren't you a history teacher at Anneville High?"

"Not today, dear girl."

The crowd jostled around them, occasionally bumping into Winter or Avery, who hadn't moved since running into each other. After the third tipsy Annevillian collided with her, Avery grabbed Winter's hand and steered her over to the now-empty origami table.

"I guess it's a good thing I cancelled my flight," Winter said once they were more or less alone.

"I really didn't mean for that to happen."

"I'm glad you're okay. I was worried when I didn't hear from you for three weeks."

"I can explain."

PART TWO

Avery, or Just Before the Fall

CHAPTER FOURTEEN

The previous February

Without warning, Meadow Lane flounced into my office, flopped into the chair opposite me and huffed dramatically. Not fully prepared for one of her snits, I opted to keep my focus carefully on the contract in front of me. At least I tried to. Once she hit me with an irritatingly melodic trilling sigh, I knew my options were limited: either I could give her the attention she felt she deserved now, or I could let her escalate her attention-seeking tactics until I could focus on nothing but her. Rather than delaying the inevitable, I closed my laptop and favored her with one of my unctuous producer smiles, the one I reserved for pop stars like Meadow, who brought as much grief as gross.

She folded her spindly arms across her chest (effectively nullifying the heavy lifting of her overpriced push-up bra) and flipped her well-coiffed blond hair in obvious irritation. Clearly, I'd offended her, but I was willing to go to my grave without learning how.

"We need to talk." She punctuated her demand by snapping her gum, and I imagined it landing in her signature blond locks (with no help from me, of course). Knowing her, though, she'd inspire a generation of young women to shave their heads or start sporting wads of bubble gum as accessories.

"I thought we had an appointment scheduled for Monday," I countered, hoping to appease her ego with the idea that our meetings were important enough for me to remember without consulting a schedule or an assistant.

"Okay, but you're not busy, right?" Snap went the gum.

"Even if I was," I said, knowing she'd take it in the exact opposite way that it was intended.

"Good." She shifted in her seat, her excitement almost palpable. "I have an idea for the next album." She blew a sizable bubble that sent a distinctly pink and fruity aroma wafting over me when it burst.

"Right on time, too, since we've already recorded five songs."

"Christmas," she said, apropos of nothing, and threw her arms out as if presenting a marquee. Meadow's manicured talons flashed in the air as she gestured in her excitement.

At my stunned silence, she repeated her minimalist pitch (complete with more fervent swinging of her arms).

Slowly (too slowly for the princess of pop, who began twitching in her eagerness), I formulated a response. "Why?" Lackluster, I knew, but I couldn't have been more dumbfounded if she'd said she wanted to record an album of shrieking toddlers accompanied by a vuvuzela orchestra.

"Meadow," I started but again fell silent as she stared at me, daring me to quell her recently acquired taste for sleigh bells.

Honestly, would any amount of levelheadedness win an argument with a woman named Meadow Lane? That was a stage name, of course, and a troublesome one at that. Not that I blamed her for longing for something different than what her parents had saddled her with. I mean, can you imagine the worldwide indifference to songstress Geraldine Spatchcock? No matter how great her voice was (and it was genuinely exceptional), that name simply inspired no appreciation.

The trouble was in picking her new name, and believe it or not, Meadow Lane was the absolute best that we could agree upon. At first, she wanted to go by Pop Star. She thought it would be like a self-fulfilling prophecy. Not that she called it that. Her words were more along the lines of "It's like making a wish that the whole world grants." I thought it would be mocked mercilessly and begged her to pick something else. We went through several iterations of her original idea, including Poppy Icon and Blast Luminary. That's when I took the thesaurus away from her. We finally settled on Meadow Lane because that's the street she grew up on, and I had lost the will to argue.

Thankfully, her talent was worth the rest of the baggage she came with (and continued to accumulate as her star rose). The more fans she acquired and the more her record sales grew, the less tethered to reality she became. Still, without her ambition and the whim of fate that helped me stumble upon her at an open mic night, I never would have ended up in a career that I love. Producing certainly wasn't on my radar when I first left home for New York, and now I couldn't imagine another job more suited to me. I had a lot to thank her for. But that didn't mean I was going to let her throw all our hard work away on a seasonal whim.

"Do you really think it's the right time for a Christmas album?" I asked as gently as possible.

"Of course not. Christmas is, like, ten months away." She spat her gum in the general vicinity of my trash can while I resisted the urge to beat my head against my desk.

"I mean, the right time in your career."

"Do you think my fans don't like Christmas?"

"I'm sure many of them do," I answered, struggling with diplomacy. "But I also think they want more of what you've been giving them. Love songs. Breakup songs. Happy songs that they can dance to, right? There's no reason to mess with success."

"Oh." She jutted her chin out, and her eyes flicked to the awards lining my bookcase (which my mother would have called it an etagere, because why use a simple, straightforward term when pretentious vocabulary existed?). "Well, I still want to do it. I think it will be fun."

"Yeah, fun and fatal. Christmas albums are for people whose careers are falling apart."

Now she was the silent one. I felt bad for being so blunt, but I had work to do and zero time to coddle her ego.

"Do you think I'm not good enough to pull this off?" Her voice seemed unusually small, and I felt a momentary twinge of guilt.

"Of course you are. You're one of the best singers I've ever met," I reassured her. "Why don't you take some time and really think about this, okay?"

"Right now, I'm thinking that maybe it's not *my* career you're so worried about, and maybe you need to do some thinking too." With that, she rose and sauntered to the door. Despite being indoors and several floors up (at twilight, no less), she slid on a pair of designer sunglasses, tossed her hair once more, and strode out the door.

I stared at her retreating backside for a few moments as her words sank in. What did she mean by that? Surely, she wouldn't end our working relationship over something as trivial as a Christmas album. Would she? I knew that Meadow could be sensitive and more than prone to overreactions, but I really was looking out for her best interests. And that shouldn't mean she would abandon me over a minor disagreement. Not after all we'd been through together.

We'd met almost a decade earlier in one of those accidental moments that makes even skeptics stop questioning fate. I'd been set up on a blind date with someone who was apparently even less thrilled by the prospect than I was. I sat alone at a bar for over two hours alternately losing myself in the numerous people-watching opportunities and convincing myself that my supposed future bliss was simply nervous or time-challenged or lost at the opposite end of the city. Eventually, I forgot all about my would-be rendezvous and allowed myself to enjoy the open mic night (that my matchmaking friend apparently considered atmospheric for a first date). The alcohol I'd consumed hadn't hurt either.

I admired the courage of the performers who took the stage, showcasing their talent (or lack thereof), and ended up staying long after I should have accepted that I'd been stood up. I was just about to leave when the most gorgeous voice I'd ever heard stopped me. On the stage stood an awkwardly shy blonde, practically hiding behind the microphone stand and the curtain of hair that fell across her face. She wore an oversized cardigan and loose-fitting jeans, one more element of her camouflage. In short, she had zero stage presence, but the voice almost made up for that.

As she sang, the noise of the crowd died down as conversations stopped and patrons turned toward the small stage, focusing all their attention on this awkward waif, and the more time she spent on that stage, the more she came into her own. I watched in utter amazement as her confidence built along with her song.

After she left the stage, I introduced myself and bought her a drink. I had no real agenda when we started talking, but by the end of the conversation, we'd concocted a reckless plan to record an album—her songs and that voice were more than a sure thing, so I offered to produce the album for fifty percent of whatever profit it made. If the album made nothing, so did I (which seemed fair given my theretofore theoretical producing skills). Four albums later, our partnership was profiting more than ever. True, our relationship lately was less "team," more "long-suffering coworker," and yes, Meadow's ever-expanding squad of sycophants kept trying to drive us apart, but we both recognized the potency of our collaboration. Surely, this would be no different.

I tried returning my attention to what I'd been doing before Meadow had breezed in and upended my world, but my mind was definitely not in the right place. I was just about to call it a day when my phone rang.

At the sound of my best friend's voice, a wave of relief washed over me. Abby had been my lifeline all throughout my childhood (as I had been for her). We didn't talk nearly as often as we used to (usually because I was too busy), but at that moment, I wanted nothing more than to get lost in a conversation with her. I didn't even care what we talked about so long as it wasn't my apparently lackluster career or anything related to the music industry.

"How's that goddaughter of mine? Has she conquered the world yet?"

"Right now, she's working on conquering her science project."

"I'm sure she'll do great," I said, not confident at all that I was right. Juno was smart, I knew that much, but somewhere along the way I'd lost track of her aptitude for science. Or math. Or the arts. Clearly, I'd fallen a bit behind in my godmothering.

"That might have been the case if she'd started the project two weeks ago when it was assigned instead of waiting until the last minute." Abby's volume increased, probably for the benefit of her daughter. I guessed that tactic worked about as well on Juno as it had on her mother.

"Tell her there's a Nintendo Switch headed her way if she crushes this." To be honest, I'd probably get her one even if she didn't do that well. She could drown her sorrows in gaming just as well as she could celebrate her victories.

"You don't have to do that," Abby said.

"But that's the beauty of being the godmother. I get all the fun and none of the responsibility."

"That's not even a little bit accurate."

"But it is fun," I countered as I added the most expensive option to my online cart. "What accessories do you think she needs?"

"Avery, stop," Abby snapped. "I don't want to bribe my daughter to do her homework. Besides, she'd rather see you than add another expensive toy to her collection."

"That's not true," Juno called out in the background.

"That's a great idea," I said, ignoring her materialistic commentary. "Why don't you guys come for a visit the next time she gets a break from school? I'll put you up in a hotel, or you can stay with me." I opened a new tab on my laptop, making plans for a visit that had yet to be confirmed. "We can go the complete tourist route or not. We'll see what you're in the mood for."

"Actually, I was thinking it might be nice if you came to see us instead."

For the second time that day, I was at a loss for words.

"Your goddaughter is forgetting what you look like."

"I look a lot happier in New York."

"But the half-marathon I'm running is here."

"In Anneville? There's not enough town to fill a 5k, let alone a half-marathon."

"It's a charity run." She barreled ahead, ignoring the slight against our hometown. "I'm raising money to fight lupus. I thought you might want to be a part of this. I'm running for Aggie."

"Of course I'll donate," I said, dumbstruck by my friend's selflessness.

"I was hoping you would play a more active supporting role. Maybe you could help Juno cheer me on." I could picture her shrugging almost meekly, like she knew what she was asking of me but expected me to do what she wanted anyway.

"I wish I could, Abby. I'm just not ready to be in that place again."

"The place where you support your best friend? Or the place where you actually show up for Juno?"

"When have I ever not shown up for Juno?"

"Any time you could send money instead. Which is every time she's needed you here."

"Ouch."

"The truth hurts. I have to go. My daughter needs more than an ATM can offer."

The line went dead, leaving me reeling, again. Rather than stay in my office to lick my various wounds, I decided to take a walk. I hoped the time outside would clear my head, but if that failed, there was always clarity at the bottom of a glass.

CHAPTER FIFTEEN

I hadn't given my hasty departure much thought beyond escaping before my mother called to complete my trifecta of aggravation. Not that we communicated regularly (or at all), but if ever she decided to rekindle our relationship, this would be the day. So, with my self-preservation in mind, I started walking, not really caring where so long as I put distance between me and my problems. As I weaved along the crowded sidewalk, dodging oblivious tourists and hyper-focused professionals fleeing work as the week drew to a close, I noticed the cold wind only long enough to zip up my coat and stuff my hands in my pockets. Otherwise, my thoughts were decidedly elsewhere.

I couldn't say I was exactly surprised by Meadow's little outburst. That was just Meadow being Meadow. In the years we'd worked together, she'd drifted steadily away from the shy and uncomplicated young woman I'd ushered into the limelight. Sadly, I'd grown accustomed to her threats (idle or otherwise). I didn't necessarily want to welcome the end of our working relationship—all the headaches aside, she was still the most talented (and profitable) artist I worked with—but at that moment, I wouldn't have been all that sorry to see her go.

Her not-so-subtle dig at my career, however, had caught me somewhat off guard. True, it had been a while since I'd added any awards or accolades to my collection. Also true, of late I hadn't been quite the phenom I'd been dubbed when my first collaboration with my incipient diva topped the charts. But to suggest that I was worried about *my* career rather than hers? She had that all wrong.

Unpleasant as that conversation had been, it paled in comparison to my disagreement with Abby. We'd known each other almost as long as we'd been alive, and I honestly couldn't remember a time when we weren't best friends. Certainly, we'd quarreled before—that was bound to happen in thirty-plus years. But it was always over something trivial like what to do on another dull Friday night in Anneville. Or what lie to tell our parents about what we did instead of spending another dull Friday night in Anneville. Those dustups always blew over quickly and never called the very foundation of our relationship into question. But there she was this afternoon, a thousand miles away, doing exactly that.

She knew how busy I was and how hard it was to get away. She'd known that before Juno was born, before I became her godmother (the "god" part of which I was completely unsuited for, another fact Abby had known at the time she asked). She also understood why I hadn't been back home in well over a decade, or at least I thought she did. But I must have been wrong since she was casually asking me to roll back into town for her half-marathon debut.

Could I drop everything and visit Anneville? I'd have to rearrange some things, but it could be done. And it would make Abby happy. But what if I ran into any of the reasons I'd left home (namely, my parents)? As far as I knew, they still lived in town—Abby would have told me if they'd moved—and the town was microscopic. Just enough room for a church, two schools (elementary and high school), a post office, and a lot of backward thinking.

A car horn blared beside me, startling me out of my thoughts and back to the present that I'd been successfully avoiding. The sun had completely set, taking what warmth it had offered with it, and my hands were frozen. Apparently, my coat pockets were no match for the icy wind swirling around me. I needed to warm up and maybe try to put this day behind me. Fortunately, it seemed that while I'd been lost in thought, my feet had their own agenda. They'd followed the familiar path to one of my favorite bars, The Ski Shop. The bar itself was nothing special, but it was close to home, the bartenders were skilled and not overly friendly, and best of all, none of my exes was likely to show up there. Friday night unfortunately meant karaoke night, but I thought perhaps it might be worth it to get out of the cold. If not, I could retreat to my apartment just a couple of blocks away.

A gust of warm air welcomed me as soon as I opened the door. I blamed the inexplicably popular karaoke night for the mass of bodies I had to fight through to reach the bar where, thankfully, one seat was open. Normally, I would avoid wedging myself between two strangers, but my legs were tired, and it wasn't like I had a wealth of options. I dropped wearily onto the vacant stool, resisting the temptation to lay my head on the bar. I hadn't even had a chance to think about removing my jacket when the woman beside me uttered something that was lost to the cacophony of the bar. I wasn't exactly in a chatty mood, but curiosity got the better of me. I asked the woman to repeat herself, and as soon as I laid eyes on her, I stopped regretting my choice.

Her red hair looked a little wild, as if she, too, had recently blown in from the blustery outdoors, and I swore I saw her blue eyes twinkle. That was probably wishful thinking, or maybe it was thanks to the ever-present Christmas lights strung around the bar. Either way, they were enchanting, and I suddenly felt a little off-balance. An endearing blush dusted her freckled cheeks, and she seemed almost surprised when I asked her to repeat herself.

"I asked if you're having a rough day. Because you seem like maybe you are." She cleared her throat, and the blush deepened.

"I was. At least, I thought so, but now it seems like I might have been mistaken."

I couldn't tear my eyes away from her, a feeling that seemed to be mutual, and we sat there staring at one another silently (perhaps because she didn't want to break the spell any more than I did).

CHAPTER SIXTEEN

Carl, one of the bartenders, interrupted whatever was happening between us by delivering a drink I hadn't ordered. (Not that I didn't normally appreciate such attentive service, but "charming lush" wasn't exactly the impression I wanted to make.) Once Carl was off again to tend to my new companion's rather impressive order, I took the opportunity to introduce myself, a formality that, apparently, I needn't have bothered with. I admit, I was somewhat surprised that she knew my name. Not that I wasn't a minor celebrity in certain rather small circles, but I couldn't believe that I'd previously met her and had somehow forgotten both the face and the name—Winter. I doubted I'd forget again.

She was adorably evasive about our curiously one-sided shared past, and until that moment I hadn't realized that the human capacity for blushing was so high. I might have been more alarmed if not for her obvious abashment every time she said something she thought she shouldn't have. Figuring out what connected us became a kind of intriguing puzzle, and if

I had to spend time with an attractive, disarming woman to unravel this mystery, well, that was a sacrifice I was willing to make.

Our conversation remained sporadic while we stayed at the bar, with interruptions from the bartender, from Winter's delightfully encouraging friend, and then from an unfortunate reminder of what I'd been trying to escape from in the form of a terrible karaoke rendition of Meadow's first single.

"Do you want to get out of here?" I asked her, desperately hoping she'd be willing to abandon her friends and her untasted wine in favor of spending time alone with a semi stranger. It was a risky proposition, but I didn't want this moment tainted by Meadow's unwelcome intrusion (no matter how subpar that trespass might be).

I couldn't help but smile as Winter bundled herself for our impending exploit. She took great care with each garment she added to her well-swaddled person, smoothing and adjusting each barrier to the elements. She was like a walking L.L.Bean catalog. The song that inspired our change of venue came to a blissful end before Winter finished donning her many layers and various buffers against the cold (including a completely adorable knit hat with a multicolored pom-pom and matching mittens). I could think of very few things I'd rather be doing than risking hypothermia in an ill-conceived attempt to get to know this woman better.

The night was surprisingly still, as if even the usual traffic and commotion of the city understood the importance of this moment. I almost didn't want to break the silence that enveloped us, but it wasn't like I could get to know her through telepathy. And as delightful as the night was, it was going to end eventually. The part of my brain that wasn't busy cataloging every one of her captivating features was resisting the suddenly overwhelming urge to spout clichéd pickup lines. Thankfully, Winter spoke first, saving both of us from the litany of inanities clouding my mind.

"Do you still sing?" She kept her face forward, allowing me an opportunity to study her profile.

"Only vicariously," I answered honestly before her words fully sank in. "Wait, when did you hear me sing? Is this part of your secret file on me?"

"I plead the fifth." She bit her lower lip and wrinkled her nose, almost like she wasn't sure she'd get away with keeping me in the dark.

"Why won't you tell me how you know me?"

"I promise I will someday."

"I like the sound of that." I probably should have pushed harder, but she was too cute to argue with. "There's not some dark, nefarious reason you're being so secretive, is there?"

"Of course not. It's just kind of embarrassing." She wrinkled her nose again, and, really, it shouldn't have been so endearing. Apparently, I had a thing for adorably meek women.

"Now I have to find out," I said and bumped her shoulder with mine.

That's when I stepped on a patch of ice and had one of those moments when time slows so that you can fully experience every nuance of the mishap currently befalling you. It was almost like an out-of-body experience as I saw myself on a definite airborne trajectory—the dramatic launch before the far-from-graceful landing. Meanwhile, my arms spun like windmills as I desperately tried to find something to hold on to lest my dignity take a similar dive. I hit the ground with a thud, resigned to the dwindling possibility of making any kind of positive impression on Winter.

"You were saying something about not wanting to be embarrassed?"

To her credit, Winter was kind enough not to outright laugh at my mishap, but I could tell by her expression that she was fighting the urge hard. I'm not sure I would have had the same resolve. Instead of mocking me, she gave me her mittened hand and helped me back on my feet. I confess, I took advantage of her kindness and held on to her hand even after I was steadily upright. I guess one good thing came out of my one-sided battle with gravity.

Given my recent brush with the elements (resulting in a now damp backside) and Winter's reddened nose and cheeks, I opted to steer us in the direction of some hot cocoa, a decision that Winter appreciated immensely.

CHAPTER SEVENTEEN

On the walk to the hot cocoa place, we talked almost continuously about things large and small. But whenever I brought up our disparate knowledge of one another, Winter got evasive. So, like any normal adult would, I started teasing her about it. I offered ridiculous suggestions and silly explanations for her wealth of information about me, all of which she managed to refute (though she seemed unduly flattered by the theory that she was a gingerbread-house-dwelling witch).

"I know. You're a spy."

"Why would that be embarrassing?" she asked.

"Maybe you're bad at it."

She offered me a look best described as amused exasperation and then shot me down once more. "I'm not a spy of any caliber. I'm a food stylist."

"That sounds like a fake job, a.k.a., a cover story."

By then we'd reached our destination (good news for my frozen extremities). A bell above the door jingled as a young couple exited, carrying the scent of joyful indulgence with them. I held the door open, letting Winter escape the cold first.

"How's your butt?" she asked as she passed me, probably as much out of concern as desire to be finished with this conversation.

"I've heard good things."

"Have you also heard that you're impossible?" She sounded more amused than upset.

"Nope. That's never come up."

When we sat down with our drinks a short time later, I immediately sampled mine, savoring both the flavor and the warmth that seeped into my freezing body. Winter, on the other hand, eyed her cocoa (with its mound of chocolate-drizzled whipped cream) as if deciding the safest way to approach.

"New topic," she said before savoring a spoonful of whipped cream. "What brought you to New York?"

"A bus." She shook her head, her frustration clear. Not wanting to cross the line from endearingly mischievous to outright grating, I offered a more complete answer. "Which I boarded because I thought I was going to be an actress."

"I take it that you've since changed your mind." She spooned more whipped cream into her mouth, this time closing her eyes in sheer bliss as she savored the treat.

"More like I had it changed for me." I shrugged my faux indifference. In truth, I still regretted the almost entirely downward trend of my theatre career.

At first, I'd dedicated myself to securing my place on the stage. I auditioned for any role possible. I studied the craft of acting (at perhaps a less than reputable establishment). I hired an agent, and then found a cheaper agent, and a cheaper one still. Ultimately, the only role I played with any success was that of starving actress.

"I think the pinnacle of my career and the point at which I opted to start considering other options was performing in a commercial for an over-the-counter diarrhea medicine."

"That doesn't sound so bad." For the second time that night, she suppressed her laughter.

"There was a jingle and a dance that accompanied it. It was a national ad. The entire country witnessed my flameout. For the record, it's really hard to hold on to your dignity while harmonizing about loose stool."

There was more to the story, of course, but I opted not to share the family tragedy aspects of my past. I mean, really, I'm not sure there's ever a good time to trot out the "my parents are callous, selfish louts who care more about money and status than actual humans" stories, but a preliminary date was absolutely the wrong time.

It didn't help that I landed that mortifying gig around the same time that my Aunt Aggie's palliative care began. I had no money to get home to see her before she died, though I did everything I could think of to get it, including going to my parents for a loan. But since they'd never approved of or even appreciated my relationship with Aggie, they refused. I missed the funeral for the same reason. That's when I decided I would never be in that position again.

"Your turn." I desperately needed to focus on anything else. "What brought you to New York?"

"It wasn't a bus." She winked and immediately blushed, and I didn't think I'd ever seen anything as adorable. "I already told you. I'm a food stylist."

I confessed my ignorance of food styling, and she filled me in with humorous stories of diva sauces, impossible entrées and quests for enough perfect potato chips to fill a commercial. It turned out that she visited the city for work fairly regularly (which gave me a bit of hope for future outings), but she had no interest in living here, and I had no interest in living anywhere else.

When she explained what prompted her to leave the city, I felt equal parts impressed, dumbstruck, compassionate, and bewildered. I supposed not everyone had a family best avoided, but I couldn't think of anyone I'd be less likely to make a major sacrifice for than my parents. For that matter, I realized that I wasn't even willing to make a minor sacrifice for Abby, which made me more like my parents than I cared to admit. Why else would I refuse to visit my best friend? The only thing stopping me was my selfish desire not to go back to Anneville, but she wasn't asking me to live there. I could come and go as I pleased.

I'd lost track of Winter's story once I'd gotten absorbed in my own thoughts, which didn't make me feel any less selfish in that moment. I'd neglected my drink so long that the remnants of whipped cream had congealed on the surface. I glanced around the shop, making note of all the people who weren't too wrapped up in their pasts to enjoy their time there. A group of teenagers huddled around a table talking and laughing too loud for my taste. The old woman sitting at the table behind Winter clearly held the same opinion. She frowned in their direction, doubling the craggy lines adorning her face. The track lighting shone through stark white gossamer hair that she'd swirled into a cotton-candy-like lump atop her head. She looked ready to shush the youths making such a spectacle of themselves, and I couldn't help picturing her as the head librarian in the archives of hell.

The mood had shifted dramatically, which was absolutely not the way I wanted this night to end, but I was still in a funk. I offered to get her a ride back to her hotel. Thankfully, she said she'd rather continue our walk. Apparently, I hadn't completely turned her off, and I hoped to do some damage control before the night ended.

When we reached her hotel, I didn't want to say good night, but what else could I do? Invite myself in for a nightcap? Beyond the word "nightcap" being completely cringe, I didn't want to give her the impression that I was only interested in getting her into bed. I mean, yes, obviously I wanted this to head in a more horizontal direction. Eventually. I also liked just spending time with Winter, which was an unfamiliar feeling for me.

"Can I text you sometime?" I asked and felt suddenly nervous that she'd say no.

"I'd like that." Then she did the cutest thing. She made me unlock my phone and added herself to my contacts under the name "Winter (Woman of Mystery)."

We stood silently for a few minutes, neither of us wanting the night to end. But a whisper followed by laughter behind us drew our attention to where her friends sat in the lobby staring at us. All they needed was a bucket of popcorn to make their entertainment complete.

"I should go before they get me kicked out of my hotel." She shrugged, as if getting bounced from one's accommodations for unruly friends was a normal occurrence. Then, before I knew what was happening, she leaned in and kissed my cheek. If I'd been at all clearheaded, I would have pulled her back for a less chaste good night, but before I could catch my breath, she'd turned away and was approaching her thoroughly engrossed friends.

CHAPTER EIGHTEEN

Despite more than a few serious issues in my life at that time, the one conundrum that occupied my thoughts was Winter. Who was she? Aside from being a thoroughly captivating food stylist with a big heart, I knew nothing about her. But she somehow knew me—in an apparently embarrassing way. Although, considering her proclivity for blushing, I couldn't say that last part was much of a clue. I spent the better part of the night (time that would have been better spent sleeping) replaying our time together and racking my brain for some idea of our connection. In defiance of my strenuous mental efforts, the answer eluded me.

But if anyone was likely to help me solve the puzzle of how Winter knew me, it was Abby. Except for my free time and an appreciation for our hometown, I shared everything with her. No way would I have kept meeting an undeniably gorgeous redhead to myself. Under normal circumstances (if meeting a stunning, adorably awkward, mysterious stranger in a bar could be considered in any way normal), I'd just call my friend and get some answers (along with a generous helping of grief). But knowing Abby, she was probably still upset with me and wasn't likely to help me out. Obviously, I had a problem (technically two), but I was determined to address both of my predicaments in one phone call.

"I'm still mad at you," Abby answered after prolonging my agony for an eternity while she allowed the phone to ring.

"What if I called to apologize?" I held my breath, hoping that earning her forgiveness (for a questionable grievance, mind you) would be so simple.

"I'd question your timing." I should have known better than to expect this to be easy, but I could have done without the riddles.

"Can you just put me out of my misery and tell me what that means?"

"It means that I have yet to receive whatever expensive olive branch you sent to pave the way for this phone call."

"I thought expensive gifts were the problem."

"Only when they take the place of time spent with my best friend."

"Maybe I've changed my ways." A bark of laughter rang in my ear. "I fail to see the humor."

"Not surprising. You fail to see a lot of things."

"Enough with the brainteasers. Can you just accept my apology?"

"I'd love to." I whooped (to myself) and was about to embark upon a victory dance when Abby interrupted my glee. "But I'm wondering what's different this time."

So close. "Different?" I asked with all the innocence I could muster.

"We've had this conversation before, Avery. More than once."

"And you're doubting that I've suddenly become a good listener?"

"Something like that."

I could picture her expression—a blend of disappointment and begrudging affection—as she waited for whatever excuse I would dream up. Instead of trying to charm my way out of an argument, I decided to tell her the truth.

"I met someone."

"Was it a therapist?"

"You're hilarious," I said, though, in truth, I was relieved that she was moving from anger to jokes (even bad ones). Maybe this wasn't a lost cause after all.

"Fine. Who did you meet?"

"Funny you should ask," I said and proceeded to tell her everything about my curious evening with Winter, including my frustrating ignorance of our shared history.

"You don't mean Winter Holliday, do you?"

"Possibly?" I said, regretting my nonexistent information gathering skills.

"Fabulously wild red hair, gorgeous blue eyes, freckles?"

"That's a remarkably accurate guess."

"Friendly and charming in kind of an adorkable way?"

"You are freaking me out right now."

"And you are as remarkably oblivious as ever." Rather than arguing her apparently valid point, I awaited the explanation. "She went to high school with us."

"What?"

"Yep. She was a couple of years behind us. I can't believe you don't remember her."

"I'm sure she's changed in the last couple of decades."

"But how many Winters do you know?"

In most cases, that would be a completely valid question, but I felt that my exceptions were fairly exceptional. "First of all, I never met this girl in high school, and second, I'm surrounded by people who call themselves Faddy McMoneybags and spell their names with dollar signs. My social circle is kind of skewed toward the unusual."

"Fair point."

"Thank you," I said, ready to celebrate my minor triumph.

"But there weren't that many students at Anneville High. You had to work really hard to not know someone, especially when they worked behind the scenes for your senior musical."

"What?"

"I believe she worked the spotlight."

"I do remember being exceptionally well-lit for that play."

What an ass I was. Apparently, Winter and I had a whole history that I had completely forgotten. If anyone should be embarrassed, it definitely wasn't Winter.

"She still lives in Anneville, by the way, and she's very involved with the community."

"What?" I said again, hoping for a different explanation, which was not forthcoming.

"Guess you'll be rethinking that trip back home," she crowed.

After we hung up, I dug my senior yearbook out of its hiding place. I'd been dragging that thing around with me through multiple moves and more than one decade. I should have thrown it away years ago, but for some reason, it hadn't made it to the trash. I guess nostalgia has a startling longevity, and at that moment, I couldn't have been more grateful to be a sentimental pack rat.

I flipped through the pages, hunting for evidence of my connection to Winter, and it was everywhere. Winter had made a social nuisance of herself, joining just about every club at Anneville High. I lingered over the many pictures of her, smiling broadly amongst her peers in the French club, Mathletes, the chess team, the yearbook, and more. If there was organized appreciation for something, Winter was a part of it—including the musical. I spotted her lurking on the sidelines of the big group photo, the one in which I stood front and center, basking in the rather nugatory limelight of Anneville High.

Mystery solved, I texted Winter and sent evidence in the form of that group photo.

I can't believe you remembered. She added a series of emojis to indicate her embarrassment.

I had a little help, I confessed and apologized for not remembering sooner, an apology she dismissed.

For the record, if anyone should be embarrassed it's me. I'd like to make it up to you, maybe with dinner? I'm willing to travel anywhere to make this happen.

Anywhere?

Almost anywhere. I draw the line at space travel.

Noted, she answered.

Three bouncing dots indicated she had more to say, but a message from Meadow interrupted the moment.

I found another producer who wants to make my Christmas album. We're doing lunch today to talk details. Thought you should know I don't need you to make this happen.

Shit. I couldn't not deal with this, and I couldn't maintain a fun, flirty conversation with Winter while simultaneously fighting to save my career.

Can we talk later? I asked Winter. Without waiting for a response, I turned all of my attention to ingratiating myself with Meadow, dignity be damned.

CHAPTER NINETEEN

I debated whether to contact Meadow immediately or just wait it out—her temper tantrums always came to an end. Though that end generally came courtesy of me giving in to her. For once, I wanted the give-and-take with Meadow to be less me giving and her taking. But since the chances of that happening were about as likely as Kanye West winning a Mr. Congeniality award, I knew I'd be the one to capitulate. The question was, when? If I responded so soon after she baited me, she'd think I was desperate, and that would only make future dealings even less appealing. However, if I waited, she'd assume I'd decided to let her be someone else's problem (not that she would ever refer to herself in such honest terms). She could easily spin that to her advantage with the press, and in a media battle, my only leverage was the truth, which wasn't nearly as sensational as whatever headlines Meadow would generate. Either way, she'd win.

Figuring that semiprivate frustration was preferable to becoming public enemy number one (at least as far as Meadow's legion of fans were concerned), I opted not to wait. Much to my chagrin, Meadow enjoyed having the upper hand too much to bother responding in a timely fashion, a fact she broadcast at every opportunity. She'd taken full advantage of her status as media darling to let me know just how busy she was not returning my call—in a span of three days, I'd seen no fewer than five headlines regarding her social activities, and I wasn't even seeking them out. No, she just showed up unannounced (typical Meadow behavior) and dropped a black cloud on any activity that followed. I knew her goal was my insecurity, and it didn't help that she loved the chase, as long as she was the one being pursued. Times like this, I wished I had discovered someone with a shred of humility.

Reluctantly, I sent another text to Meadow and awaited the photographic evidence of her ignoring me for the umpteenth time.

The most exasperating part? She wasn't even the woman I wanted to be chasing, but I'd spent so much time distracted by Meadow's ego that I'd neglected Winter, maybe for longer than was forgivable. To be fair, I *had* sent a message apologizing for the abrupt end to our previous conversation, so technically, it was her turn to respond. However, based on the definite lull in our communication, she didn't seem to know that.

I tried not to dwell on the numerous explanations for Winter's prolonged silence, but the recent blow to my self-esteem at Meadow's capable hands left a giant hole for doubt to creep in. What if I had upset her by not remembering her? It wasn't like we were friends (or even acquaintances) in high school, but it also wasn't like Anneville High was at risk of overcrowding. What if she was busy dealing with the foodie equivalent of Meadow Lane? What if she lost her phone or was stricken with amnesia?

"Or what if she's just not interested?" I admitted a more realistic and thoroughly more depressing explanation and instantly regretted it. I didn't want Winter to be disinterested, or worse, only interested in friendship. I wanted her to be as thrilled every time the phone chimed as I was. But a week of silence told a different story.

Then again, maybe she was waiting for me to reach out to her, and I was too busy stewing to do anything about it. Yes, I'd sent the last communication, but she might have interpreted that as a request for time to deal with work issues. Did I really want to risk losing something so promising because my pride was a little hurt? On the other hand, what if I'd waited too long? What if Winter had simply grown tired of waiting to hear from me and had turned to any of the more geographically appealing offers in Anneville?

I no longer trusted myself to sort this out. I needed help, and that meant that I needed Abby. Again. Hoping that her happiness at hearing from me so soon would override her previous irritation, I picked up my still-silent phone and called my best friend.

CHAPTER TWENTY

"Are you busy?" I asked the second Abby answered, hoping to dodge small talk.

"A single mother of a child who's never met an activity she didn't want to try? What could possibly keep me busy?"

"At least you have time for sarcasm."

"Just call me Superwoman."

I heard an excessive amount of noise in the background, like Abby was now fielding calls at pep rallies. Dismissing that thought on the grounds that it contradicted everything I knew about her, I barreled ahead with the reason for my call.

"I need help."

"On that we both agree."

"Can we save the quips until after we've dealt with my crisis?"

Her answer was muffled by the definite roar of a crowd.

"Where are you?"

"At a hockey game," she said casually, as if we hadn't spent all of high school avoiding all things sports related.

"When did you become a hockey person?"

"When Ethan Miller insulted female athletes during gym class, and Juno decided to prove him wrong. She says she's going to be the next Manon Rheaume."

"Naturally," I said, though it was anything but. Thirty seconds into this conversation, and I was already lost. "Is she any good?"

"You could see for yourself if you came to a game."

"I'll check my schedule," I said, my intention of immediately forgetting that declaration notwithstanding.

Another burst of cheering indicated that some satisfying sports thing had just happened. This was hardly the right environment for a meaningful heart-to-heart conversation. Still, it wasn't like I had a lot of other options—most of my contacts fell closer to professional connections or ex-girlfriends than confidants, and my chances of catching Abby when she wasn't engrossed in some other activity were minimal at best.

"Can we get back to my situation, please?"

"As long as you're okay with occasional bursts of earsplitting parental pride."

Taking that as a resounding yes, I filled her in on all the details of my tentative whatever this was with Winter. Even if Abby was only half-listening (which I strongly suspected after an ill-timed and thoroughly jarring howl of support for Juno), she got an earful about the many conversations with Winter that preceded Meadow's Meadowy sabotage of my private life and the subsequent collapse of communication with Winter.

"Let me see if I understand. You prioritized a woman who makes a habit of ignoring you until she needs something over someone who you might have a two-sided conversation with, and now you're worried that you've blown your chance?"

"It sounds even worse out loud than in my head. Am I doomed?"

"Only if you keep talking to me instead of Winter."

"But I can't just pick up where I left off, can I? What if I waited so long that now she won't want to talk to me?"

"A great way to find out is by turning to me instead of her."

"I trust you to be honest with me, even if it hurts."

"How do you know that Winter won't?" Another blaring cheer pierced my eardrum, suggesting that Juno had performed some hockey feat worthy of deafening anyone in earshot.

"Because she's too sweet and kind to be mean."

"Thanks for the compliment."

"You know that's not what I meant. Now quit being offended and help me."

"On one condition."

"Name it," I said immediately, without even considering the possible repercussions.

"After this, the advice hotline is closed until I see your face again."

"I don't suppose Zoom counts?"

"In person only." I was about to offer an all-expenses-paid trip to Anywhere But Anneville when she cut me off. "And I have no plans to travel anywhere any time soon."

Damn. I should have known there'd be a catch. But it was a catch I didn't have to worry about unless I needed more advice. If I could evade any crises long enough, Abby might forget about this agreement (though I knew the likelihood of either of those things happening was practically nonexistent).

"Fine," I acquiesced, cringing in mere anticipation of time spent in my hometown.

"Have you considered that she's going through the same thing? That maybe she's worried about contacting you?"

"Or she's just not interested." I allowed my pessimism to take control.

"Only one way to find out," Abby countered.

"But it's her turn."

"Are you twelve?"

"No, I'm just nervous, so I've gotten all mixed up in my head, and I thought maybe my best friend who knows me better than anyone might help me sort this out."

"I think it says a lot that you, the queen of charm and confidence, are nervous. It says even more that you're even considering what you should do. In the past you would have just said, 'Her loss' and moved on."

"So, you're saying that not knowing what to do actually means that I do know what to do?"

"Something like that."

"I can't believe I agreed to go back home just to hear that I should text Winter."

"I never said text her."

"You want me to call her?"

"Unless you think she'll respond to Morse code."

"She probably has many hidden talents."

"Well, unless one of them is eternal patience, you're in trouble. Call her."

CHAPTER TWENTY-ONE

Obviously, I valued Abby's input—not only had I petitioned for it, but I'd also agreed to a steep price in exchange for her words of wisdom (though I held out hope that I could get myself out of that promise on the grounds that it was extortion). Still, I delayed as long as possible before making the call. For one thing, I still had some work to do, and I knew that wouldn't happen if I was talking to Winter (or worse, nursing my wounds after what I surmised would be the most gentle yet devastating rejection of my adult life). But even after I'd reviewed several contracts (with more attention to detail than I'd ever exhibited) and tackled all of the budgets I had the mathematical wherewithal to tackle, I still didn't pick up the phone. In truth, I was nervous, which was an unfamiliar but oddly refreshing way to start a (hopeful) romantic entanglement.

So, I took a walk, grabbed a bite to eat and primped more vigorously than necessary (especially since the target of said primping would be oblivious to my excessive grooming). When I ran out of stalling tactics, I picked up the phone, asked any deity within earshot to help me out, and without allowing myself one more second to chicken out, I made the call.

"Hello?"

The question in her voice did little to put me at ease, which is exactly why I would have preferred to text. But I was in this now, so I breezed past that bit of awkwardness, and in all defiance of my emotional state, I hoped for the best.

"It's me," I declared before remembering that she clearly didn't know who "me" was in this instance. "It's Avery."

"Hi." Her voice warmed, and with that one syllable she erased my concerns. "I'm glad you called. I wasn't sure I was going to hear from you again."

Okay, score one point for Abby and her irritating levelheadedness.

"I've been busy with work." As soon as the words left my mouth, I wanted to call them back. Even though work had kept me preoccupied, I didn't really want Winter to think she was inconsequential. "Which was extra challenging since I kept hoping I'd hear from you."

"I'm so sorry. My phone met an untimely demise. I'll spare you the details, but a heat gun and chocolate ganache were involved."

"Now I'm intrigued."

"That was my plan." She laughed nervously. "Anyway, not all of my contacts made it to the new phone, so I've been answering my phone any time it rings, just in case it was you. It wasn't. Obviously. But I've befriended an astounding number of telemarketers in the last couple of weeks. You have no idea how many opportunities I've had to renew my car's warranty."

"And you turned them down?"

"I was waiting for a better offer." Her voice hit a low register that I felt in my stomach (and elsewhere), and suddenly the temperature in my apartment rose about a thousand degrees.

"What did you have in mind?"

"What are you offering?"

Well, this conversation was going so much better than expected.

"Come to New York. I want to see you again."

"I want that too."

"Good. So, what are you doing right now?" I knew the chance that she could just hop on a plane to come see me, especially from Anneville, which was at least a forty-minute drive from an airport, was practically nonexistent, but apparently, I'd become an optimist in the course of one phone call.

"Feeling grateful that you called," she answered without hesitation. "And now I'm blushing."

"Sounds serious. Can you multitask, or should I call back when you're not so busy?"

"You can call anytime."

The air around me felt thick and hot, and I suddenly felt tingly all over. "If it helps, you're not the only one who's glad I called."

"Oh, really?"

"Yeah, my best friend will be ecstatic."

"Are you always so…"

"Charming?"

"Pretty sure that's not the word I was looking for."

"Then you'll have to let me prove you wrong. Are you free this weekend?"

"I have to work."

"Who would ask you to work on a weekend? Can you get out of it?"

"I wish, but I committed weeks ago, and I can't back out now."

"Can I at least know what I came in second place to?" I tried to keep my tone light but feared I was crossing over into whiny territory.

"It's a photo shoot for Bader's Brats and Beyond. I'm looking at a full two days of sausages and kielbasa in Wisconsin."

"That has to be the wurst way to spend a weekend."

"Did you just dad joke me?"

"Not if it makes you think less of me."

"On the contrary. It makes you much more approachable."

That didn't exactly sound like a compliment, but her accompanying laughter—soft and sweet and something I knew I had to hear more of—softened the blow to my ego. We stayed on the phone for over an hour, talking about everything. Each time I thought she couldn't possibly be enjoying this as much as I was, one of us asked a question that launched another conversational excursion.

She told me about her first job serving up ice cream and smiles at The Swirling Dervish. If I hadn't left Anneville by then, I felt certain that the sight of her alone would have made me a soft-serve devotee. I also learned about her family (which sounded like a model of domestic tranquility, even without my family for comparison). She'd actually been sad to leave home when she attended culinary school, which was a completely foreign concept to me.

"You should let me make you dinner some time."

"Tempting. Most people are too intimidated to try cooking for me."

"That's because most people can't offer my signature blackened grilled cheese."

"Sounds irresistible." Her laughter trickled out again, and I grinned giddily, feeling a little like a teenager.

As she spoke, I pictured her lounging cozily on her couch, under a blanket with her feet tucked beneath her. Soft, flickering light from a fire in the fireplace that probably existed only in my imagination danced across her face and one shoulder that was bared when her loose-necked sweater slipped down. Of course, I had no way of knowing if any of that was true. I'd never seen Winter's home (though I couldn't believe it would be anything but cozy). For that matter, I didn't even know if she was home. She could have been at work or a hotel in a city other than mine or on a date with someone who wasn't me. And rather than let my mind dwell on that possibility, I asked the first question that popped into my head.

"Why didn't you ever talk to me in high school?"

"Right. The most invisible freshman just walking up to the most popular senior."

"You're all over the yearbook. That's hardly invisible."

"You didn't see me."

"Believe me, I regret that. And it still doesn't explain why you never talked to me."

"You mean aside from the massive crush that made me forget how to breathe, let alone speak, whenever I saw you?"

"Tell me more about this crush."

I'd been joking, mostly, but that didn't stop Winter from reminiscing about my last play at Anneville High—*Guys and Dolls*—and how she had volunteered to work behind the scenes just to see little old me. She almost lost her job working the spotlight after she missed a cue during "If I Were a Bell" because she was too busy wishing I was singing it to her.

"I wish I'd been singing it to you, too, instead of serenading Tyler Appeldoorn."

"Really? I always thought Tyler was nice."

"He was an absolute sweetheart, if only he hadn't wholeheartedly believed that liberal application of Axe Body Spray could ward off all of life's negativity."

"That bad?"

"It was like a force field. The smell still haunts me." I shivered at the memory of Tyler's cloying aroma.

"So, when am I going to see you again?"

"You could come see me this weekend."

"No matter how many times you ask, I still have to work."

"When do you have time off?" I hoped the answer would be soon, but as misfortune would have it, our calendars wouldn't align for several weeks. I didn't want to wait that long to lay my eyes (and maybe some other parts) on her, but at least we had an actual date to look forward to. Until then, I'd have to survive on texts and hours-long phone calls.

After we finally said goodbye, I saw a text from Meadow. She'd sent it almost an hour earlier, and I couldn't help my delight at keeping the diva of delays waiting for once. Even better? She and her manager wanted to meet. Fortunately for me, I seldom interacted with Malcolm, a smarmy little man who generally left me feeling like I needed a shower after even the briefest of conversations. But he always appeared when it was time to launch an album or a tour. I figured that his presence meant Meadow had changed her mind about firing me and making a Christmas album. All at once, things were starting to look up for me.

CHAPTER TWENTY-TWO

I walked into the restaurant designated as our meeting place feeling more lighthearted than time spent with Meadow and her manager, Malcolm Stewart, usually warranted. In part, I was eager to put this dispute behind us and get back to making music—the kind we could both be proud of. But I was also riding the high of regular communication with Winter. Since our marathon phone call the previous week, not one day had passed without at least a good-morning or good-night text shared between us, but it was usually more. Despite the fact that I'd never been an overly cutesy person, I found myself smiling at the silly, adorable texts Winter sent and smiling more as I responded with something even sillier or more adorable. I'd spent more time on the phone in the past week than in the previous decade, and I ended every conversation wanting more. Even now, my prosperous future with Meadow hanging in the balance, my mind was on Winter rather than the imminent fawning I'd be called to do.

Meadow was late, of course (she couldn't arrive on time if her fame depended on it), which left me with nothing but time to kill and Winter on my mind. From my seat at a small table in the middle of the restaurant, I considered whether the chic space would work as a possible venue for my upcoming (but not nearly soon enough) date with Winter. I mean, the woman was a trained chef whose entire career centered on food. I doubted a hot dog from a cart would be the way to her heart.

Before this meeting, all I knew about the place was that it had recently topped one of those "Best of New York" lists. While meeting at a restaurant seemed an odd choice for Meadow, who hadn't eaten in public in close to five years, given its newly minted status as VIP central, her choice seemed suddenly less mysterious. That girl would sell someone else's soul for more time in the limelight. Fortunately, her thirst for notoriety came with modern décor, comfortable seating, and an impressive menu.

I'm at Juniper Rose waiting for my meeting to start, and all I can think about is whether you'd like it.

I've heard great things, but I've never been.

We'll have to change that.

Her immediate answer let me believe that I was on her mind as much as she was on mine. But before I could say more, a crescendo of voices clamoring for Meadow's attention (the telltale sign of her arrival) drew my awareness to the door.

Forty minutes after I'd expected her, she casually strolled into the restaurant, stopping several times for an autograph or a selfie with a fan. She didn't even feign regret for her extreme tardiness. Malcolm twitched nervously in her shadow, trying to usher her along faster, to no avail. I admit, I enjoyed watching his repeated failures.

Despite the gray gloom that had obscured the sun for days, Meadow had donned her ever-present sunglasses. Nevertheless, I knew that roughly a pound of makeup lurked behind those lenses, an unnecessary bit of window dressing, and one that came at Malcolm's slippery suggestion. What had started as a bit of mascara "to make her eyes pop" had snowballed into a ninety-minute beauty regimen, the results of which were questionable at best. And with each layer of cosmetic "improvements" added, a bit more of Meadow's genuine personality disappeared, as if to make room for the new (and decidedly worsened) version. Somewhere under all that makeup was the young woman I'd met all those years ago—sincere, compassionate, and a little insecure, not in her own talent but in the world's willingness to embrace it. I held out hope that she'd reemerge one day soon.

Malcolm, overdressed for the occasion in a three-piece suit, ran his fingers through what remained of his wispy blond hair. His perpetually reddened face revealed his spiraling irritation with his client's attention to everything but his repeated directions. I tried not to laugh—I'd endured a similar frustration on multiple occasions—but I couldn't think of anyone less deserving of my sympathy.

Half an eon later, they landed at the table, and after much fussing, settled themselves across from me, a task that would have been far less complicated if Meadow had looked up from her phone even once. Clearly, there was some social media emergency that took precedence over minor decisions like her future. As if it wasn't insulting enough to be ignored, her disinterest ensured that I'd be dealing with Malcolm for the bulk of the conversation.

We exchanged terse greetings before he got down to business. "Thanks for meeting us on such short notice, Aves." He smiled in his reptilian way.

"My pleasure," I lied.

"Meadow tells me you're not interested in the Christmas album. That's a real shame."

"For whom?" is what I wanted to ask. Instead, I focused on the one person whose opinion actually mattered to me. "Did you tell him why?"

She paused her texting long enough to shrug in my general direction.

"I'm not interested in doubts and obstacles." Malcolm waved his hands in the air above the table, as if he could erase my concerns. "I want results."

"Even if the result is a blow to Meadow's career?"

"Let me ask you this, Aves. How many Christmas albums have you produced?"

"At least as many as you," I challenged him.

"You're cute." He winked, and my skin crawled. "But you're also inexperienced. You have no way of knowing this won't be a hit."

"It's a mistake, whether you believe me or not, and I can't in good conscience support this."

"Turns out, we don't need your support." He smiled again, all teeth. "Reg Burundi is already on board to produce if you don't come to your senses."

"Reg Burundi?" My voice hit a degree of shrillness usually reserved for dealing with my parents. "He calls you Meadow Lame. He said your last tour was as lively as wet cardboard. Why would you ever agree to work with him?"

She shrugged again. "And we both got tons of media attention. It doesn't mean anything."

I was glad we hadn't gotten around to ordering. I'd completely lost my appetite.

"This meeting was just a courtesy," he said.

"Doesn't feel all that courteous."

"We could have done this over the phone, but Meadow thought you deserved a more respectful approach."

I stared at the back of her phone, feeling anything but respected.

"I'll leave you to your bright future." I scooted my chair back to depart, dignity intact. But as I rose from my seat, I collided with a waiter holding a tray overloaded with mixed drinks, none of which escaped Meadow's gravitational pull. I watched as multiple glasses flipped in the air like gymnasts in slow motion, their contents sticking the landing on Meadow, dousing her hair, her designer outfit and, worst of all, her phone, in a rainbow assortment of frozen cocktails.

Her subsequent shriek hit that high C she was famous for, and all at once every cell phone was trained on us. Never one to let an opportunity slip by, Malcolm wasted no time loudly accusing me of intentionally sabotaging his client, as if I'd perfected the art of punitive clumsiness. Meanwhile, Meadow and I tangled over one another in our awkward attempts to blot the many stains adorning her outfit. It was like a sticky, nightmare version of Twister, all caught on film by no fewer than two dozen bystanders.

"You can forget about working with Meadow ever again," Malcolm announced loud enough for diners in the restaurant down the block to hear. Then he whisked a still-dazed and blotting Meadow to the door.

She paused at the threshold and cast an almost apologetic glance back at me before Malcolm dragged her outside, and I waited for the media bombardment to begin.

CHAPTER TWENTY-THREE

Once the commotion died down and the cell phones disappeared, I apologized to the poor waiter who'd been caught in the celebrity crossfire, tipped him a hundred dollars for his trouble, and left without looking back. I wish I could say that I left with my head held high, but the last thing I wanted was to give some amateur paparazzo the opportunity for a close-up of my defeat. Even though a walk would have helped clear my head, I couldn't get away from Meadow's aftermath fast enough. I hopped in the first cab I saw, ready to put that whole scene behind me. I hoped there wouldn't be aftershocks from my incredibly public breakup with Meadow, but I didn't really see myself coming out of this unscathed.

As the city passed by outside the cab, I overthought the last hour, considering all the possible negative outcomes. Best-case scenario—Meadow's legion of loyal fans would smear my reputation all across the Internet. I stopped short of imagining the various hashtags involving my name, but that hardly curtailed the downward spiral of my overactive imagination. By the time I exited the cab in front of my apartment building, my worry on a decided upswing, a text notification interrupted my catastrophizing.

How did the meeting go? I want to hear all the details.

I couldn't say I was surprised to hear from Winter, whose capacity for thoughtfulness seemed almost boundless.

Disaster isn't a strong enough word. I might have to go into hiding. Maybe change my name. Does the Witness Protection Program take walk-ins?

My phone rang less than a minute after I sent my text, and in spite of my sullen mood, I couldn't help but smile at the sound of her voice.

"What happened?" Her voice was concerned and comforting. I wanted to get lost in it and forget about whatever fallout was headed my way.

Even so, her genuine sympathy surprised me—not that I didn't expect her to be compassionate. I just didn't think my little career hiccup warranted such concern. I almost brushed it off— why waste valuable phone time with Winter on unpleasantries? But something in the tone of her voice compelled me to share all the details of my recent ignominy, but not before pouring myself a drink and flopping onto my couch. By the time I got to the spilled drinks portion of my downfall, anxiety had crept back in, and even though I knew I'd regret it, I opened up my laptop and began searching for coverage of the event. It took no time to find pictures of me pawing at a shocked and soaking Meadow with captions calling me everything from a creep to a perv. And the comments were merciless. Worse, Meadow and Malcolm had already blasted their skewed version of events in the press and across social media, complete with unflattering hashtags and the pronouncement that Meadow's working relationship with me was on permanent hiatus.

"This is a nightmare," I whined.

"Who pays attention to that stuff anyway?"

How I envied her innocence.

"So far, ten thousand eight hundred and fifty-two people have reacted to this post alone."

"Well, I never pay attention to that stuff."

"And that's why I like you more than all those other people."

"I thought it was my air of mystery that you liked so much."
At the sound of her lovely, tinkly laughter, I decided to simply
enjoy the one thing in my life that seemed to be working
out, more or less. I closed my computer and gave her my full
attention.

"It wasn't entirely a dumpster fire," I said, grasping for a
glimmer of Winter's optimism. "I did find a place to take you
for dinner when you visit."

"I was promised burnt grilled cheese. You can't get a girl's
hopes up and then not come through."

"It's blackened, not burnt. I'd make it for you right now if
you were here. Why aren't you?"

"Because someone has to make the six-foot-tall papier-
mâché rabbit and giant chocolate egg for the Anneville Easter
Eggstravaganza."

"Easter isn't for another week."

"This is my practice egg."

"Are you working on it as we speak?" I asked, as if an
enormous confectionary dry run was in no way unusual.

"The chocolate is setting, so now I'm focused on the
oversized basket to hold the egg. The grass is all wrong, though.
It keeps coming out more turquoise than green."

"Is this a standard evening for you?"

"It's not un-standard."

CHAPTER TWENTY-FOUR

While I appreciated Winter's complete lack of interest in the often-devastating world of social media (she was a definite port in the storm of scandal surrounding me), I couldn't very well stay on the phone with her forever. Not even until the populace latched onto a juicier bit of gossip about some other unfortunate star (or star-adjacent figure like myself). Nor could I treat my apartment like a Fortress of Solitude, hiding out until the coast was clear. No, I had to deal with the aftermath of Meadow and Malcolm being less than impeccable with the truth.

The blowback started small enough, so small that I shrugged it off at first. An up-and-coming band I'd been courting suddenly backed out of our next meeting—the one with the contracts to sign. When I tried to reschedule, they told me they were going in a different direction. They didn't come right out and say that my alleged misbehavior with Meadow had nudged them in that other direction, but I had my suspicions, especially when two other acts suddenly had creative differences before we'd even started creating. I knew I was in trouble. I just didn't know what to do about it.

Obviously, I wanted to repair the damage to my public image. But even if I asked nicely, Meadow and her hired character assassin weren't likely to recant the convenient lies they'd spread as far as the Internet reached, especially when she was garnering so much sympathy in exchange for the defamation of my character. They'd transform Meadow's alleged suffering into multiple double-platinum albums in Malcolm's shady hands. The upside to that, I supposed, was that I still got royalties from every album she sold on the back of my now worthless reputation.

I considered telling my side of the story, but to whom? Reporters weren't exactly knocking down my door to get the less glamorous truth, and though I was no slouch at public relations, my skills were the David to the Goliath that was Malcolm and Meadow's well-oiled media presence. I didn't stand a chance. Beyond that, I understood all too well that the more a person denied a public accusation, the less likely the public was to believe in their innocence. Plus, I really just wanted the whole thing to go away. So, I did nothing. I avoided social media and all its unkind talk about me. Not that acquaintances didn't feel obliged to share the stories with me. I heard all about my mistreatment of Meadow and others, including artists I'd never even met. Worse, someone with nothing better to do than cause me grief circulated rumors about my failed acting career, suggesting, of all things, that I'd traded sex for roles. I guess it didn't occur to them that the stellar lack of professional acting gigs on my resume contradicted that claim.

At least I didn't have to worry about Winter reading some splashy headline about my fictional dalliances. She didn't follow celebrity gossip, and I certainly wasn't going to share the so-called news with her. Why would I introduce such an unpleasant topic into our conversations, which were otherwise delightful? Not that I didn't think she would be sympathetic—her gentle, understanding nature was one of the things I liked best about her. I just didn't want to taint the remaining good part of my life with all the ugliness from the rest of it.

So whenever we talked, I evaded questions about me by turning the conversation back onto her. That way, I avoided delving into the unpleasant details of my downfall, I got to learn more about her, and I got to enjoy that weak-kneed, fluttery-stomach, warm-all-over feeling that seemed to appear whenever I heard her voice (the seductive qualities of which were only magnified by her incognizance of just how sexy it was). It was a win-win-win.

"You haven't talked about work much lately," she said one night when we both should have been sleeping.

"My work isn't very interesting." That statement had more truth to it in the moment than I cared to admit. "I'd rather hear about you."

"I do makeovers for lettuce. You hobnob with celebrities."

"Celebrities are overrated and much less interesting than lettuce."

She was starting to catch on to me, though. One night, after sharing an amusing story about her recent time as the Anneville High Hammer, she said, "I never talk about myself this much. I want to hear about you."

"I'm just a failed actress slash record producer. How can I possibly compete with the Anneville Hammer?" I deflected once again.

Since I had nothing better to do than avoiding any hashtags with my name attached and counting down the days until I saw Winter in person, I started somewhat obsessively planning for that visit. The itinerary I created accounted for at least thirty hours of activity each day, not including certain hoped-for distractions. I booked her a room at the Carlyle, hoping all the while that she'd want to stay with me—not necessarily in any kind of lusty way (not that I'd refuse if things headed in the direction of the bedroom). I just wanted to spend every second we had together, which would be easier if we stayed in the same place.

I was still searching for flights for her when she texted that she'd already booked one. I couldn't help but grin that she was looking forward to our time together as much as I was. But before we got carried away with tantalizing discussion of the most long-awaited, highly anticipated first date in the history of courtship, her client demanded her attention. It only made me look forward to our good-night call all the more.

Still riding the high of our conversation, I busied myself with some of the mundane tasks I'd ignored since my scandal-induced hibernation began. After all, I couldn't very well entertain a VIP like Winter with my apartment looking like Oscar Madison was my decorator. Not that I was living in squalor, but it had been a minute since I'd done any tidying—I'd been a bit preoccupied by watching my career go down in flames. Unopened mail had piled up on my coffee table. Some takeout cartons had taken up residence on my counter, and I'd all but given up on laundry and any attempts to keep it contained. I didn't anticipate making the space immaculate in one day, but it felt good to sort through the clutter and restore order to my home.

I was still reveling in the delight that always came from talking to (or thinking about) Winter when my phone rang. I didn't even check to see who was calling before I answered, expecting to hear Winter's voice. Instead, I heard my name in a small, shaky voice. Juno. I could tell she was fighting back tears, trying to be brave, and without warning, shock and worry replaced the joy I'd felt just a moment earlier.

"Mom's hurt." In the background, I heard the unmistakable wail of a siren. "It's bad."

"I'll be on the next flight."

CHAPTER TWENTY-FIVE

I spent the better part of my trip to Anneville worrying. Thanks to the succinct nature of Juno's call, I had no idea what had happened to Abby, but my imagination had no problem filling in the blanks. By the time I landed, I'd put her through everything from a sprained ankle to a near decapitation. I stopped short of actually killing off my best friend, but as her imaginary injuries increased, so did my concern about Juno.

Her father was out of the picture (which was a blessing), and her grandparents were sweet but living the retirement dream in Florida. That left Juno alone and unsupervised in a fairly grown-up situation. Not that I didn't think she could take care of herself, but I worried that other well-meaning adults didn't know that. I had visions of her being dragged off by social services, doomed to some kind of nightmare Dickensian existence. I didn't know what to expect when I finally made it to the hospital, but whatever predicament greeted me, I had the sinking feeling that I wouldn't be ready to handle it.

I'd given up on formal religion right around the time that an allegedly benevolent god bestowed the gift of lupus on my one hundred percent wonderful aunt while my less than twenty percent decent parents remained the picture of health. Even so, I wasn't above supplication for Abby's benefit. Not to mention Juno. We would both be lost without Abby.

For a small-town hospital, Anneville Memorial boasted an overabundance of areas devoted to the painful task of staving off heartbreak. I barged into the tenuous comfort of three different waiting rooms before wandering into the correct place almost by accident. Much to my relief, Juno hadn't been left alone during her ordeal. An avuncular fellow sat beside her, sharing a bag of chips and hopefully comforting words. As he shifted in his seat, the fluorescent lights gleamed off his bald spot surrounded by a donut of salt-and-pepper hair, and Juno actually smiled at whatever he said, further reassuring me. I hated to think how lonely and terrifying it must have been to wait for news about her mom, even with an adult assigned to her.

She'd grown since the last time I'd seen her. A lot. That shouldn't have surprised me as much as it did. Nearly three years had passed since we'd spent time together in person. In that time, she'd blossomed from the determined little kid in unruly pigtails that I remembered. Her wavy light brown hair now hung loose, falling well below her shoulders. But she still had a baby face, freckles and all, and her full eyebrows lent an air of added seriousness to her stern expression.

She stared at me wordlessly for a moment, her eyes glassy with tears. I still needed some kind of information beyond Juno's ominous words: "It's bad." I almost turned to the gentleman who'd been keeping her company for answers, but Juno finally found her voice.

"There was an accident during the race."

"That was today?" I'd completely forgotten about Abby's big athletic endeavor.

Juno frowned at my interruption. "Mm-hmm. She fell hard."

"You saw it?" She nodded and looked away. No wonder she wasn't eager to share the details.

"That must have been scary," I stated the obvious, earning a scoff.

When the responsible stranger finally left us alone, we settled in for a long wait. Juno opted to entertain herself by staring straight ahead rather than acknowledging me, which I tried not to take offense at. The silence between us wasn't exactly awkward or painful, but it wasn't comfortable either. I hoped to distract her from her intense focus on the wall across from her—rather bland in its once-trendy off-pink wallpaper which couldn't have been less interesting if it was a documentary on wallpaper. Surely, a conversation would be more engaging than the entire lack of activity on the other side of the room. We used to talk all the time when she was little. Granted, that was when she was just a kid and bodily functions were the height of comedy. Now that she was a mature thirteen-year-old, I doubted flatulence held the same appeal. But what did thirteen-year-old girls talk about? I was hoping to find out.

"How's school?" Admittedly, that wasn't the greatest start to a meaningful conversation, but my mind was a bit preoccupied with my best friend's medical emergency.

"Why do adults always ask about school?" Clearly, she was peevish.

"Would you rather talk about your investment portfolio?"

An epic eye roll was her only response. Really, she probably burned three hundred calories simply by expressing her disdain. And then, just in case I didn't catch on to her indifference, she returned to staring at the wall.

"Remember when we used to talk to each other?"

"Remember when you were a part of my life?"

Ouch. I supposed that I deserved that. "I know I haven't been around much lately."

"Try at all."

"But I'm here now."

"For how long?"

This kid was brutal, but she had a point. "Honestly, I don't know." That depended on Abby's injuries and whether I had any work to return to.

"At least you're honest."

"Hey, I've never lied to you, and I'm not going to start now. We're in this together, so maybe give me a chance?"

Her response fell somewhere between a shrug and a nod, and though I had no reason to, I felt marginally better about the situation.

More than a couple of hours later, we were allowed to see Abby, but only briefly, which was both too much time and not nearly enough. Bruises marked her face as well as the side she'd fallen on. There were some lacerations as well but none so bad they required stitches. She was pretty out of it from surgery and the rest of her ordeal, so conversation was erratic at best.

"If you wanted me to visit, you could have just asked," I joked, trying to make light of a ghastly situation.

"Tried that. Didn't work."

Juno clung to her mom, a heartbreaking blend of worry and sadness on her face. Even after the doctor explained that recovery would take several weeks but Abby would be fine, eventually, Juno maintained her tight grip. It was next to impossible to convince her to leave her mom there for the night and go home with me. I couldn't exactly blame her for her reticence. The responsible adult she was used to had been traded in for a new and completely inexperienced model. Even I wasn't confident about my skills as a caregiver, but I had no choice but to do it.

CHAPTER TWENTY-SIX

I held no illusions that I was cut out for parenting, even on a temporary basis, but I had no clue just how ill-suited to the role I was. Since Juno was already housebroken and well past the perpetually sticky phase of childhood, I thought that looking after her would be like hanging out with a friend who had algebra homework and couldn't drive, but from the start, she seemed to take pleasure in proving me wrong.

Abby had sent us home with clear instructions: eat something and get some rest. I had every intention of living up to those minor expectations. Juno, on the other hand, showed no interest in helping me achieve that goal. When I asked what she wanted for dinner, she shrugged her indifference before turning her attention to her phone. No problem. I'd had decades of experience deciding what was for dinner. Finally, my expertise would pay off.

"How about pizza?" I went with a tried-and-true option, sure to please even a teen testing the limits of my patience.

She shook her head no. "Mom would want us to have something healthy. Plus, the only good pizza place in town closed last summer."

That didn't bode well for my success, but I could recover. "Burgers and fries? I'll even spring for milkshakes."

"Red meat is an environmental blight. It's totally destroying the atmosphere."

"Well, then we can have chicken." She looked up from her phone long enough to frown at me. "Let me guess. Chickens are responsible for microplastics in the oceans."

"Doubtful. But I only like chicken when it's in something, like chicken tetrazzini."

"I don't suppose there's a chicken tetrazzini emporium in town?" A look of pure incredulity crossed her face. A definite no. "Fine. We'll have popcorn."

Without giving her the option to rebut my decision, I headed to the kitchen and set about preparing our dinner, which I cooked on the stove like the responsible adult I was. If Juno appreciated my culinary efforts, she didn't let on, but since she joined me in the living room for trash TV instead of skulking off to her bedroom, I considered the evening a minor victory.

The situation didn't drastically improve overnight. If anything, Juno managed to shine a spotlight on my failings at every opportunity. I thought I was earning points by letting her stay home from school the Monday after her mother's accident, but she didn't go for it. She said it would be easier not to worry about her mom if she was worried about her classes instead. Dubious reasoning, if you asked me, but I wasn't going to forcibly prevent her from getting an education.

"Do you need a ride?" I asked, despite the fact that, even if her school was on the opposite end of town, she could still walk there in under twenty minutes.

"No, but I do need lunch."

"Lunch?"

"You know, that meal in the middle of the day? The one between breakfast and dinner."

"Thanks for clearing that up for me. I'll be sure to make a note."

She stared at me expectantly for a moment. "You did make me lunch, didn't you?"

I didn't want to admit defeat so early in the morning, but there was no way around it. Not only had I neglected to make her lunch, but I also had nothing on hand that I could pass off as an intentional meal. So, I did the next best thing. I handed her cash and promised to be more prepared the next day.

"Fifty dollars? It's a school cafeteria, not Le Cirque."

"Then I guess you'll have change for me when you get home." By her expression, I knew that was the last I'd see of that money.

I watched her walk as far down the block as I could see. Five or six houses down, a bubbly blond girl joined her, increasing Juno's vivacity by about a thousand percent. I told myself that it was good that she had friends, and then the panic about successfully meeting my obligations set in. Clearly, I had a lot of work to do, starting with meals.

I did try talking to Abby about her daughter's epic grudge holding and flair for dismissing any and all attempts to tend to her needs. If anyone could help me appease her monumentally stubborn daughter, it was Abby. Unfortunately for me, she was feeling no pain (or any connection to reality) thanks to some high-quality medication. Essentially, she muttered something incomprehensible at me before falling asleep. If I was going to make any progress with Juno, it would be without the aid of my best friend.

An hour later, as I pushed a shopping cart with one broken wheel haphazardly through the aisles of a supermarket two towns over, I contemplated my options. I could continue to supply Juno with cash and snack-food dinners, but she seemed rather unimpressed with those lackluster efforts so far. If I wanted to impress her (and I didn't not want to), I supposed that I could call for backup in the form of Winter. Not only could she supply us with palatable food that held more nutritional value than cardboard, but I'd also get a chance to reconnect with her. It had been more days than I cared to count since we spoke.

The monumental appeal of that plan notwithstanding, I doubted I'd earn much credit with Juno for simply making a phone call. Winter would get all of the praise (rightfully so), and Juno's antipathy toward me would continue as if I hadn't contributed to her well-being at all. That left me with only one option—doing the work to prove myself to her.

So, I filled my rickety cart with ingredients that I would somehow assemble into meals. The frozen dinners called to me like Sirens, but I resisted their premade allure, hearing Juno's litany of objections in my head as I headed toward the produce section. I did, however, grab a couple of packages of Oreos. Even if Juno turned her nose up at them, I felt certain I'd need the fortifying qualities of chocolate to get me through the coming weeks. In spite of considerable effort on my part, the situation did not magically improve the next day, at least based on Juno's unenthusiastic reaction to the lunch I packed for her.

"What is this?" She frowned at the contents of the bag I'd handed her, then sniffed the food and grimaced.

"It's lunch. You know, that meal between breakfast and dinner?"

She didn't appreciate my humor nearly as much as I did. "But what is it?" The look of horror had yet to leave her face.

"It's sushi. I made it myself."

"Sushi?"

"You don't like sushi?"

"Not after it's been sitting in my locker for four hours."

I hated to admit it, but the kid had a point. And I didn't have time to prepare anything else. Grudgingly, I took back the emblem of yet another failure and forked over more cash.

"We're having sushi for dinner," I called after her as she headed out the door.

Somehow, I managed to screw up lunch every day that week. She couldn't have peanut butter and jelly because of another student's allergies, and she refused to even entertain the idea of a hot dog. By Friday, I spared myself the frustration of making anything and just handed her more money. I didn't even care that she'd easily profited off my culinary ineptitude. I just wanted her to warm up to me a little.

With that thought in mind, I decided to change tack. If I couldn't wow her with my efforts in the kitchen, then I'd turn to the healing powers of presents. When she arrived home from school on Friday (late, but I let that slide), I proudly showed off the arcade game I'd totally overpaid for. But it had four different games and was sure to provide hours of fun if she ever relinquished her obvious disdain.

She merely frowned in the direction of the machine, not even entertaining the thought of a friendly competition. Instead, she muttered something about her homework and headed upstairs to her room.

As I stood alone in the living room, the sounds of Ms. Pac-Man ringing in my ears, I realized that grand gestures weren't going to cut it. If I was going to get back in good standing with my goddaughter, I'd have to prove that I was worth her trust.

CHAPTER TWENTY-SEVEN

After almost a week in the hospital, Abby finally came home, doubling my workload but drastically reducing my solitude. Even when she was sound asleep, she was better company than her daughter. To be fair, Juno was perfectly willing to help with any tasks related to her mother's well-being, a fact I may have exploited to get the bathroom cleaned. But her attitude toward me didn't improve as rapidly as her mother's health (which was incredibly slow going).

Unfortunately, Juno's demeanor wasn't my sole concern, because on top of the longest snit in teen history, I was also concerned about my floundering career and Abby's recovery depending on my care—I couldn't even manage to pull together lunch for a thirteen-year-old. How was I supposed to nurse a semi-invalid back to health while also juggling all of the adult responsibilities I'd avoided up to that point?

The short answer was that I wasn't. I took to sleeping on an air mattress beside Abby's bed in case she needed anything during the night. The fact that the air mattress had celebrated more than a score of birthdays and had the slow leaks to prove it meant that I spent more time succumbing to gravity than actually sleeping, and I had the bags under my eyes to prove it. I should have bought a new one, but that seemed like I was setting down roots and making my stay in Anneville more permanent than I cared for. I'd stick around as long as Abby and Juno needed me, but then it was back to city living for me.

The days didn't treat me any more kindly than the nights. I spent my mornings scrambling to tend to everyone's needs and failing spectacularly. Between bickering with Juno about her mercurial dietary preferences and trying to balance the grooming needs of three females in a one-bathroom house, I invariably overlooked some important task or another (usually my own cleanliness). One morning, as I broke down in tears over a cereal bowl I couldn't fit into the overloaded dishwasher that I'd neglected to run for three days in a row, Abby called out to me.

I dashed to her, expecting to discover her splayed on the floor writhing in agony, only to find her still in bed, casually surfing the Internet on her laptop.

"You rang?"

She glanced up and hit me with what I can only describe as the ultimate concerned mom look.

"How many days has it been since you took a shower?"

I opened my mouth but couldn't even formulate a response. There I was, panicked that she'd reinjured herself on my deficient watch, when all she wanted was to discuss my hygiene.

"That's not a question you should have to think about." Her expression softened. "I love that you're here, and I appreciate everything you're doing for us, but you don't have to do it all."

"I don't?" This was news to me. "You're a handful. Who else is going to deal with you?"

"How about her?" Abby pointed to her screen, where a visibly chipper brunette smiled broadly.

Pepper Cavendish, home health aide. Even her picture exuded capability. As much as I wanted to be the hero of this little family, I also wanted what was best for Abby, which was definitely not my pathetic nursing skills.

"I'll make some calls while you're in the shower." She picked up her phone, but before she had a chance to dial, I gave her the most gentle yet heartfelt hug I could offer. Of course Abby would take care of her caretaker.

It took some time and effort, but once Pepper started, life became more manageable, in most respects. My housekeeping skills didn't necessarily improve, nor did my cooking. But I couldn't say I was sad to have someone else helping Abby with the more personal aspects of her care. We'd been friends for decades, but there were some lines I really didn't care to cross. Helping Abby on and off the toilet was definitely one of them. Abby seemed equally relieved to hand that responsibility over to a virtual stranger.

My appreciation for Pepper wasn't entirely altruistic, however—her help meant that there might be some free time at some point in my future. Maybe then I could take care of some important things I'd neglected in favor of being a good friend. While I didn't completely mind the distraction from my public castigation, I did need to try to salvage my career and reputation at some point. I also hadn't talked to Winter in longer than I cared to think about. Not that I didn't want to. She was constantly on my mind when I wasn't sparring with Little Miss Malcontent over peanut allergies and missing homework. Several times, I started to send a text or even call, but the easy distraction of Winter would only give Juno one more reason to be angry with me. But even if I wasn't worried about Juno's reaction, reuniting with Winter there in Anneville seemed like accepting defeat.

The only one who wasn't thrilled about the new arrangement was Juno. She showed Pepper nothing but kindness and respect (thanks in large part to her mom's flourishing recovery under Pepper's care). I, on the other hand, endured a decided uptick in Juno's extraness. One night, when I asked for her help clearing the table after a dinner that she sulked through, she sighed dramatically, rolled her eyes, and then carried her still-full plate to the kitchen. I bit my tongue (an increasingly challenging task) until she left the kitchen, heading in the opposite direction of the still-messy dinner table.

"Stop," I called out. "That table doesn't look clear to me."

She spun around to face me, arms folded across her chest, her expression pure defiance. "Why do you care? I don't even know what you're still doing here."

"What does that mean?"

"You found somebody to take your place, so just leave. That's what you want, isn't it?"

"Not that I need to defend myself, but hiring Pepper was your mom's idea."

Her features immediately softened, and her arms fell to her sides. "What?"

"I'm not trying to leave. I'm trying to do what's best for your mom, which, let's face it, is not having me as a caregiver."

A trace of a smile played at the corners of her mouth. "That's true."

"You're stuck with me for a while, kid," I reassured her, and it was like she finally accepted that I didn't have one foot out the door. Her smile grew, just a little.

"Do you think we can get Pepper to cook for us?" She headed back to the dining room and resumed clearing the table. "She can't be any worse than you."

"Don't push your luck."

CHAPTER TWENTY-EIGHT

Once the antagonism between us dwindled, we were like a force united in driving Abby up the wall. One or the other of us was always right by Abby's side, eager to help in any way possible but usually getting in Pepper's way as she provided actual assistance. Our combined hovering only intensified once Juno's school year ended. Instead of doing whatever kids did in the summer these days, Juno spent all her free time by her mother's side, tending to her every need (or at least attempting to). Between the professional caregiver and the amateur team, Abby didn't have a moment of alone time or peace. Even when we weren't in the same room as her, we were lurking on the sidelines, pestering Pepper for updates. We should have anticipated a meltdown.

One weekend in early June, as I put the finishing touches on Abby's breakfast, Juno asked her mother for the millionth time if she needed anything. She'd taken to second- and third-guessing Abby's candor regarding her own well-being. I could detect the cracks in the armor of her patience, but Juno either lacked that perceptiveness or was blinded by her concern. Whatever the cause of her obliviousness, she pushed her mother too far, and we both paid for it.

"Stop." Abby's harsh tone caught Juno off guard. She froze, mid-pillow-fluff, and her eyes widened in fright. "I need you both to stop smothering me. I know you care, and I appreciate all you've been doing, but I need a break." Her expression softened, and she took her daughter's hand in hers. "You should go do something fun. Enjoy your summer. Please."

"What if I don't want to?"

"Then I'll reverse ground you."

"I don't even know what that means." Juno easily dismissed the reprimand. Her posture and expression were pure defiance, as if Abby's words had no real power over her.

"It means that you're forbidden from entering the house until nightfall."

Her jaw actually dropped at the threat, and she stood there, speechless for a moment. For just a minute, I wished that I'd possessed that power back when my every word butted against Juno's attitude. Now, however, I felt bad for the kid and wanted to ease what surely must have been a blow to her equilibrium.

"You've got a brand-new bike in the garage." That was another of my attempted bribes. "You should give it a test drive."

Abby turned her serious gaze on me. "The reverse grounding applies to both of you."

"What? Where am I supposed to go?" It wasn't like I could hop on my ten-speed and pedal around town.

"I don't care what you do. I just need some peace from both of you."

Even if I crawled, it wouldn't take until nightfall to tour the entire town. Beyond that, I'd successfully avoided going anywhere in Anneville other than Abby's house and the hospital. Why would I change that now? And it wasn't like the neighboring towns were any more exciting. I was basically locked in an entertainment void.

"There's an event at The Anneville Tap," Juno suggested somewhat sheepishly. She flashed her phone at me, as if a split-second glance at the information was all I'd need to agree.

"I know I'm not exactly a paragon of responsible adulthood, but even I know that a bar isn't an appropriate place for a thirteen-year-old."

"It's actually a pretty family-friendly space," Abby said, challenging my perfectly reasonable objection. "Kids go there all the time for town events."

"I'm not sure that makes me feel any better about The Tap. Or Anneville."

In truth, I felt equally trepidatious about both places, for good reason. I hadn't been to The Anneville Tap since I was sixteen and my aunt ran the place. Back then, I spent more time at the bar than I did at home. I'd stop there after school and do my homework at the bar while Aunt Aggie tended bar and handled the day-to-day business of running the place. She'd give me free pop or water, and between customers and math problems, we'd talk about whatever was on our minds. She encouraged me to audition for my first play when I was a freshman, and she made me believe I was talented enough to be more than a high school theatre star.

My parents didn't necessarily approve of their daughter spending all her free time in a bar, particularly a lowbrow establishment like The Tap, but they didn't make a fuss as long as my grades didn't slip, and I didn't embarrass them. That was an impossibly easy standard to maintain, especially since all the regulars knew me and knew how important that time was for both me and Aunt Aggie. No one bothered me, and I got to spend time with my favorite person while avoiding my least favorite people. It was an ideal situation.

At least it was until curiosity got the better of me. I'd never even considered trying to sneak any alcohol—I didn't want either of us to face the trouble that was sure to bring. But in my junior year of high school one day when everything that could go wrong did, I succumbed to the allure of the adult Slurpee machine. On more than one afternoon, I'd ignored my homework in favor of watching the mesmerizing swirling of the bright blue and green slush. It looked even better pouring into the small glass I grabbed when Aggie was distracted by something in the back of the bar. I just wanted a little taste, nothing that would even be noticed.

But one little taste turned into a bigger one, and then I had to see if the green side was as delicious as the blue, and by the time my aunt made it back behind the bar, I was feeling no pain. Unfortunately, the issue Aunt Aggie was dealing with in back was a phone call from my parents, who chose that time to show an interest in my whereabouts. They were on their way to pick me up for some important-to-them event, and when they arrived, they found their sixteen-year-old daughter face down in her history textbook. And that was the last time I set foot in The Anneville Tap.

I had no desire to break my years-long streak of eschewing the scene of my youthful disgrace, but Juno had made up her mind. I didn't want to disappoint her so soon after our reconciliation, and we had to go somewhere. So, against my better judgment, we headed to The Tap, which had changed considerably since my last visit. Whoever owned the place now had remodeled away all of the dive-bar coziness, giving it a much more upscale pub feel. I couldn't help but look for the slushie machine, but as I turned my head to find it, I ran directly into Winter, who didn't look nearly as happy to see me as I would have hoped.

Throughout my story, Winter's focus never shifted from me. At first, I appreciated her attention, but the more I explained myself, the more ridiculous I felt. Did I really have a good excuse for neglecting this woman? At the time, I thought so, but there in the face of her sympathetic gaze, I doubted my reasoning. Looking for any way to avoid eye contact, I grabbed one of the squares of colored paper set out for origami. In my nervousness, I began folding it according to the instructions. It was more a way to avoid eye contact than an effort to create anything, and it absolutely served its purpose. By the time I finished my story, I had mangled several bits of paper and had started on another when Winter's hand on mine stopped me.

"Thank you for telling me. I'm sorry this has been such a hard time for you."

"You're not mad at me?" I held on to her hand like a lifeline.

"Oh, I'm mad, but that doesn't mean I can't be compassionate. I still don't understand why you didn't just let me know that you were going through something and needed a little time to sort it out."

"Because I knew that if I let myself turn to you, I'd never want to stop."

I risked eye contact. She definitely wasn't happy with me, but behind the anger, I thought I detected the tiniest glimmer of happiness, which I naturally took credit for.

"I'd like to make it up to you, if you'll let me."

She took half a lifetime to answer, and though I couldn't blame her for carefully considering her options, I also couldn't bear the thought of her saying no. Or the wait to hear her answer. I was a nanosecond away from darting out the door when she gave my hand a little squeeze.

"Okay, on one condition."

"Name it."

"You let me do the planning."

"That doesn't seem like me making this up to you."

"I'm giving you a second chance, and you're going to give Anneville a second chance."

As much as I hated the idea of opening my mind even the tiniest bit to Anneville's alleged charms, I hated the idea of saying goodbye to Winter even more.

"I'm in."

PART THREE

A Sumner Holliday

CHAPTER TWENTY-NINE

Winter was nervous. That made sense, she supposed. She hadn't been on a real date since her disastrous attempt at wooing Enid Horvath, the town's only mail carrier. It wasn't that she'd been heartbroken by their astounding incompatibility or even that she had given up on romance. Simply put, she'd exhausted all her dating options in town. Beyond that, this wasn't just her first date in a long time, it was with Avery—Teenage Winter would never forgive Adult Winter if she screwed this up. And there was so much riding on this one outing. Not only were they *finally* going on a real date, but she was also trying to sway Avery's opinion of the town.

Which was why, against her better judgment, she consulted Gabe about the date—no one could showcase Anneville's charms more effectively than he could. His advice would come hand in hand with his opinion, but wowing Avery was worth the acerbic backlash. She knew without question that he would have reservations about her planned reunion with Avery, especially since she'd spent so much time lamenting Avery's inexplicable absence. But now that it was explicable, she was fully prepared to pick up where they left off and see where romance took them. She hoped to bring Gabe to the same conclusion through the persuasive power of a hearty breakfast. So far, her plan was failing spectacularly.

They sat in Winter's kitchen, where she plied him with some of his favorite foods and discussed her current romantic dilemma. Gabe, however, was stuck in protective friend mode. Rather than celebrating Winter's good fortune, Gabe was hung up on the past and Avery's thoughtless behavior.

"You're doing what?" Gabe gestured with his fork, coming dangerously close to decorating her walls with hollandaise sauce.

"I'm trying to plan the perfect date for me and Avery, and I want your help."

"My help would be advising you to rethink that plan."

"Think of it like this—if I go on this date and it's a flop, then I'll get her out of my system and never have to wonder 'What if?'"

"What if the date goes well?"

"Isn't that what we should be hoping for?" Gabe remained uncharacteristically silent, but his expression spoke volumes. "Just say what you're thinking."

"She has a habit of disappearing, and I'd rather she do so without breaking your heart."

"She explained why she stopped answering me, and I've moved on. I really wish you would too."

"Unlike me, you have a habit of being far too understanding. And I have moved on. To the part where you find someone else."

"Like who?" It wasn't like there was an overabundance of local women to spend her time with, despite Gabe and Noah's remarkable ability to manifest potential love matches from what amounted to a single-and-available-lesbian desert.

"Anyone who won't ignore you as soon as life gets a little challenging." His tone softened ever so slightly. "You deserve better, and I won't let you forget that."

"Duly noted. Now, if you were trying to show off Anneville's best side, what would you do? I have ideas, but I can't decide if they're good enough."

He sighed heavily. "When are you planning on seeing her?"

"I'm hoping for this weekend, but I haven't let her know that yet."

"You might want to be sure she'll still be in town before you do too much planning." She frowned and reached for his plate, which he protectively moved closer to himself. "Obviously, downtown Anneville is where all the charm happens. Assuming she hasn't departed because it's too challenging to be an adult, you'll want to start there—maybe coffee and a muffin at the coffee shop before taking the scenic route down Main Street to the farmers' market."

She loved perusing the fresh produce available at the weekly market, especially on a sunny summer morning with the beautiful blue sky as a backdrop. There really wasn't a more picturesque Anneville moment. She didn't know if Avery would have the same appreciation.

"She's a city girl. Do you really think she's going to be impressed by farm-fresh produce?"

"Well, if she hasn't run screaming for the hills, you can whip up one of your fabulous dishes to take to the movie in the park that night."

"You don't think that's too small town for her? I want her to enjoy what Anneville has to offer." In truth, she wanted Avery to want to stay, but she didn't dare speak those words to anyone else.

"Honey, you changed my mind with some eggs. Imagine how persuasive you could be with a picnic."

He had a point, as usual, and snark aside, he'd planned the perfect Anneville outing for them. Now, she just had to hope that Avery found it as perfect as she did.

* * *

The proposed exoneration of Anneville aside, I was anxious and impatient for my date with Winter. I woke up two hours earlier than usual and spent that time hunting for something even remotely nice to wear, an almost impossible task thanks to my hasty packing for this trip. I hadn't exactly predicted an extended stay, and I definitely hadn't anticipated any social outings, especially one as important as this. That lack of foresight left me with jeans and a plain V-neck T-shirt that I didn't even remember buying, let alone packing. Considering the projected length of Abby's recovery and my protracted exile from my wardrobe, I definitely needed to go shopping.

As instructed, I met Winter at Anneville Coffee and Sweets, an establishment that had appeared during my lengthy absence. The coffee shop could best be described as cutesy, a quality that did little to sway my opinion of the town. With its minty green exterior and scalloped trim around the roof, it looked a bit like an ornate dollhouse. The large front window revealed an interior with even more color and just as much personality as the outside. The employees bordered on ecstatic, with broad, toothy smiles on full display as they dashed about in their pastel aprons, dishing up coffee and pastries with speed and efficiency. The tantalizing aroma that wafted past me each time the door opened gave me some hope for what lay ahead.

I beat Winter there by a wide margin and had plenty of time to look around, so I parked myself on a bench (another addition to the now quaint downtown) and marveled at all that had changed. Gone were the creepy pawn shop and the Anneville Diner (which took the "grease" in greasy spoon far too much to heart). In their place I found a dog groomer and a bookstore—a thoroughly shocking development from a town renowned for its lax attitude toward literacy. Beyond that, Pride paraphernalia was strewn about the downtown area like garland at Christmas time: flags dangled from the light posts on Main Street, and several businesses proclaimed their support with an impressive assortment of decals and banners displayed in their front windows. Even more unbelievable, not one window had been smashed in protest. There were no hateful slurs spray painted anywhere, and the townspeople I saw seemed entirely unperturbed by the influx of queer visibility. Either I'd woken up in an alternate reality, or Anneville had become kind of progressive in my absence. When I finally caught a glimpse of Winter heading my way, I couldn't help but watch her approach.

She strolled casually toward me, greeting people as she passed them. Everyone seemed to know her. She looked casually stylish in jeans (that fit her extremely well) and a summery blouse, the open top buttons of which offered an enticing glimpse of bare skin. She'd put her hair in a fishtail braid that hung over one shoulder, and her smile brightened as she approached the bench where I sat, mesmerized by her beauty.

"I hope you're hungry," Winter said and held the door to the coffee shop open for me. I entered that pastel refuge from good taste without hesitation.

Once my eyes adjusted to the assault by interior decorating, I skimmed the menu, more interested in Winter's nearness than my growling stomach. Even a cursory glance left me with questions. "What are baton bagels?"

"The owners are new to town and really took Anneville to heart." She shrugged as if that explained anything.

"So they took it out on poor defenseless bagels?"

"They've given everything Anneville-appropriate names, like the mallet muffins, or the pound cake, which is terrific."

I wanted to argue the merits of confusing customers with a perplexing homage to a weird little town in the middle of nowhere, but I remembered that I was supposed to be giving Anneville a chance. So, rather than risk upsetting Winter five minutes into our date, I purchased two coffees and some pound cake and asked her what was next.

We enjoyed our surprisingly delicious coffee as we strolled down Main Street, our shoulders occasionally brushing. Winter wouldn't tell me where we were going, despite my best efforts to get the information out of her. All she'd tell me was that I was in for the perfect Anneville Saturday. That hardly sounded promising, but it couldn't be all bad if we got to spend the day together. Winter acted as tour guide as we walked, pointing out all the things that had changed since I left, and I had to admit that most of them were improvements. At one point, I actually got so caught up in noticing small things about the town—like the hammer-shaped door handle on the hardware store—that I didn't realize we'd reached our destination, the Anneville Farmers' Market.

"Your plan is to win me over with grocery shopping?"

"This is only the first part of my plan. And the farmers' market isn't just grocery shopping."

I remained unconvinced, but I probably would have agreed to almost any activity if it meant spending time with Winter. "I'm curious to know what the rest of the plan is. What could possibly follow getting up close and personal with produce?"

"Come with me and find out." She took my hand and led me into rural paradise.

Almost immediately, we were immersed in completely foreign territory for me. There were more fruits and vegetables on display than I knew existed (generally, I stuck to the basics of the produce department, and even that happened infrequently). I had to admit that the offerings here looked about a thousand times more delectable than what I was used to picking through at the grocery store. And they smelled amazing. I was half an inch away from burying my nose in a basket of raspberries when Winter decided to introduce me to Hubert Henderson, a nattily dressed older gentleman whose infatuation with the carrots bordered on alarming. He clutched a bunch in one hand, gesturing with them as he praised their size and color. I wondered if he was in some sort of root vegetable appreciation society, but Winter remained unfazed by his enthusiasm. She even exchanged recipes with him, as if raving about vegetation was totally normal behavior that should be rewarded.

When Hubert eventually wandered off on the hunt for some equally stimulating pea greens, Winter continued shopping as if nothing out of the ordinary had happened. Meanwhile, I wondered if I'd stumbled into an alternate reality. But then Winter slipped her hand in mine, and I forgot all about Hubert and his unrestrained love of carrots.

The rest of our time at the market continued in much the same fashion. We picked up several items, and all along the way, Winter socialized with the other shoppers at the market. Everyone adored her (how could they not?), and she seemed to appreciate every Annevillian we encountered, quirky and otherwise. Though Winter never failed to introduce me, I preferred to watch her as she interacted with the parade of people seeking her input on everything from recipes for corn to issues with upcoming events. No matter how the conversations began, every person walked away smiling. I might have been jealous of all the attention she gave to others, but she always turned back to me, her smile growing when our eyes met.

"Are you ready for part two?" she asked after a lengthy discussion of peppers with Pastor Briggs.

"Where in town can possibly top this?" I teased. Truthfully, I'd enjoyed myself more than I'd thought possible.

"I was thinking my place."

"Lead the way."

CHAPTER THIRTY

Winter's house was mostly as I had imagined it—a standard Anneville half-duplex but with splashes of color and cozy touches everywhere. The big surprise was her kitchen, which was almost daunting in its size, not to mention the equipment it housed. She'd made some updates from a typical kitchen, including a massive stove with six burners (which was five more than I'd ever used). I also spotted several gastronomical gadgets that I vaguely recognized from various restaurants and cooking shows (though I remained clueless as to their function). Had I considered myself even remotely adept at preparing food, it might have been intimidating, but knowing my skillset (such as it was) allowed me to appreciate the magnificence of the room as an innocent bystander.

"What can I do?" I asked, hoping for an answer along the lines of "Make out with me."

"Just unpacking these bags would be a huge help."

Alas, another dream unrealized.

"I can do more than take stuff out of bags." Despite the enormity of the kitchen, we stood enticingly close.

"Like what?"

"I'm a whiz with a can opener."

"A woman with hidden talents. I like that." She bit her bottom lip, and then all I could think about was her mouth. The air between us was charged, and I felt myself leaning closer to her. "But I'll have to put your skills to use some other time."

She stepped back, leaving me dizzy in her absence. Against every impulse I had, I did as I was asked, divesting the bags of their mouthwatering offerings and carefully arranging them on the counter for easy access. Our hands touched once or twice as Winter grabbed the items she needed for what she planned as the next phase of our date, whatever that might be (I'd never been on such a carefully constructed date before, but I had to admit that I was enjoying the suspense). She stopped when she saw the bouquet of flowers I'd set beside the mushrooms.

"Where did these come from?" She closed her eyes and inhaled the scent of the flowers. Her smile sent a little fluttery dip to my stomach.

"I saw them when you were talking to Millie Seymour about the potholes on Peach Street." After my time at the farmers' market with Winter, I now possessed more operational knowledge of Anneville than I had considered possible (and though I would never admit this to anyone, I didn't completely object). "I thought you should have them."

"I'll have to thank Millie."

"Don't bother her. She has potholes to tend to. But if you really want to show your appreciation, I would be willing take on that burden."

"How selfless." She kissed my cheek, her breath tickling my ear, and told me to sit while she worked.

"I deserve more thanks than that. Did you see the size of that bouquet?"

"Some things are worth waiting for." She bit her bottom lip again and winked, at which point I just about died.

Kiss deprivation aside, I was content to watch her work her culinary magic. The kitchen filled with a heavenly aroma as she chopped and diced and did other things with a confidence that was beyond attractive. It was thrilling to see her in her element—creating several dishes so effortlessly (at least as far as I could tell). She didn't even look at any recipes. She just seemed to know what worked.

I didn't take a seat as she'd suggested. Why would I put more distance between us, especially when she looked so good? As she stirred the contents of a saucepan, I leaned over her shoulder to watch. Her breath caught when my body pressed against her. Had I intentionally tried to distract her? Who can say? Did I take advantage of the distraction? Absolutely.

"What's this?" I pointed to a bottle on the counter, ignoring the label that clearly explained its contents.

"Balsamic vinegar." Her voice caught a little.

"What are you going to do with it?"

"I'm making a balsamic glaze for the strawberry bruschetta." Over her shoulder, she favored me with a look that was equal parts amused and annoyed.

"How do you do that?"

"Preferably with fewer distractions."

"Are you sure you don't mean more?" I trailed a finger up her arm, feeling pretty pleased with the shiver and goosebumps left in my wake.

"You are incorrigible." She turned around into my arms, but rather than rewarding my persistence with her lips on mine, she told me to quit interrupting, then guided me backward to a chair.

Patience wasn't one of my strong suits. I was more an instant gratification kind of girl, but there was something to be said for appreciating the captivating behind-the-scenes view. Did I mention how well her jeans fit? Winter bending to use the broiler was a transcendent experience.

"Can I ask you for a favor?"

"Is it to stop staring at your ass?"

"No, I think I'm okay with that." She looked over her shoulder and offered an enticing little shimmy.

"I don't normally bestow favors until the second date, but for you I'll make an exception."

"Flowers and a favor all in one day? Aren't I lucky?"

"The second luckiest person in the room. What can I do for you?"

"I want to visit Abby."

I had expected something more challenging, like regrouting her bathroom or ending our date without getting to kiss her. I hardly considered it a favor to introduce her to my best friend. I actually looked forward to them meeting.

"I'd like that too."

"Good, because I feel just awful about her injury. I'd really like to apologize. And maybe offer some atonement in the form of baked goods. Do you know what her favorite pie is?"

She had no reason to feel bad—she hadn't even been in town when Abby was hurt. But of course Winter would react with over-the-top sympathy to an accident she had no part in. I couldn't allow her to feel guilty, so in a clear violation of Winter's orders, I went to her and gave her a hug. Just a comforting connection with no sexy ulterior motives. Even so, I couldn't help but notice how well our bodies fit together.

"I get the sense this won't deter you, but you don't owe Abby an apology, edible or otherwise."

"Does that mean you don't know her favorite pie?"

"I'll have to ask." She started to step back out of the embrace, but I held on.

"I have to get back to work, or we'll be late for part three of our date." Her eyes locked with mine, and there was that charge in the air between us again.

"Can't this be part three?"

She softly shook her head no. I thought maybe I could sway her with logic or some much more compelling kissing, but she evaded me.

"Not yet," she said, though her eyes held promise. "You can pour some wine if you'd like, but no matter what, we leave in an hour."

* * *

Winter couldn't tell if her plan was working. She felt certain that the date was going well, especially after the smoldering looks Avery had been sending her way all afternoon. It had been almost impossible not to give in to temptation and kiss her right there in her kitchen, movie in the park be damned. But her goal was twofold, and as satisfying as that total lack of self-control surely would have been, it would have left Avery with an incomplete portrait of their shared hometown. Even as they picnicked in the park, savoring the meal as well as the scenery, she couldn't tell if Avery's attitude toward Anneville was softening at all.

For her part, Avery had kept her promise—or so it appeared—and had given the town another chance. She'd been nothing but sweet and attentive all day. She'd been cordial—friendly even—to the townsfolk they'd encountered, and Winter had caught her smiling as they walked down Main Street hand in hand while she pointed out the most promising updates to the town. Undoubtedly, Anneville couldn't compete with New York in most areas, but Winter would take a summer night in Fletcher Park, sharing a blanket and food with the most gorgeous woman she'd ever seen, over the crowded city any day.

They'd selected a spot toward the back of the crowd, spreading their blanket under a magnolia tree, the fragrant pink blooms of which hung heavy on the branches. Despite the scores of people milling about, narrowly avoiding their picnic area, Winter barely noticed anyone but Avery. Her appreciative moans with every bite of food delighted Winter in more ways than one. She lost track of time, space, and reality just watching Avery's mouth—when her tongue darted out to lick an errant crumb off her lip, Winter almost forgot to breathe. Somehow, she maintained her composure long enough to pack up the leftovers, leaving nothing but a few inches of plaid blanket between them.

"You should come over here where it's more comfortable." Avery leaned against the trunk of the tree and patted the blanket beside her, but Winter took the invitation further, seating herself between her legs and leaning back against her.

"You're right. This is more comfortable."

As the sun sank below the horizon, taking its warmth with it, Winter wished she'd thought to bring a sweater. She shivered, whether from the chill or from Avery's nearness, she couldn't say, and then Avery wrapped her arms around her.

Avery's voice in her ear asked, "Is this okay?"

"It's perfect." She sighed contentedly. She didn't think a night could be more magical.

She forgot to pay attention to the movie, preferring to focus on the moon and the stars and the warmth of Avery's body. She'd almost missed this opportunity—so much had come between them, but something kept bringing them back together. She would never not be grateful that she'd given Avery another chance.

Just when she thought the night couldn't possibly get any better, Avery started singing along with Shirley Jones, the lyrics to "People Will Say We're in Love" caressing Winter's ear. Her voice was soft, just for Winter, and the last of her resolve melted away. She craned her neck to face Avery.

"I love when you sing. I always have."

For just a moment, neither of them moved. The crowd faded away, and the air around them hummed. Winter's gaze fell to Avery's perfectly kissable mouth—her lips parted slightly and quirked up in a smile, inviting Winter closer. Their breathing slowed, the scent of the magnolia and the wine on their breath mingling for a torturous second before their lips finally met. What began as a soft, almost tentative kiss rapidly intensified. When Avery's tongue danced across Winter's lips, she immediately reciprocated. At some point, she turned herself around, sitting in Avery's lap, her hands in her hair as their kiss deepened. A moan escaped when Avery's hands reached her ass. Her hand was an inch from Avery's breast when an exaggerated cough nearby brought them back to reality.

"So worth the wait." Avery touched her forehead to Winter's.

"Oh my god, yes. And I've been waiting twenty years." She couldn't resist another kiss, not as mature as its predecessor but still entirely moan-worthy. "What are you doing next weekend?"

"Hopefully more of that." She nipped at Winter's lip.

"Definitely. But first, I think we should go to the Pride festival."

"Anneville has a Pride festival?" Avery looked shocked when Winter nodded. "This I have to see."

"It's a date," she said and lost herself in Avery once more.

CHAPTER THIRTY-ONE

After the movie (the finale of which I completely missed in favor of devoting all of my attention to Winter), we were in no rush to join the herd of chattering townsfolk making their way out of the park. Little by little, the crowd thinned as parents carried sleepy children wrapped in blankets, and couples young and old meandered blissfully away from the park. We stayed rooted to our spot under the tree, my arms around Winter, her head on my shoulder, and watched them all go. I might have stayed that way all night, if not for the Anneville Beautification Committee starting their cleanup. A swarm of aggressively cheerful townspeople in matching A.B.C. T-shirts descended upon the formerly serene premises, armed with trash bags, recycling bins, and a can-do attitude. Before Winter had the chance to grab a trash picker and join the tidying, I packed up our gear, took her hand, and led her away from one more chance to help out.

Once we were a safe distance from the volunteer opportunity, I slowed our pace considerably. I didn't want the evening to end, but I knew that it would once I delivered Winter safely to her house. And though I suspected that our good-night parting would be sublime, I was in no rush to get there, so I walked at roughly the same pace as Winter's elderly neighbor. (Granted, Miss Opal was spry for eighty, but her fleet-footed days were definitely in the rearview mirror.) I'd never enjoyed a walk through Anneville as much as that one, Winter's hand in mine, a sky full of stars twinkling above us, and boundless possibility ahead.

"I was thinking, a week is a long time to go between dates." I broke the comfortable silence between us.

"It really is."

"We should do something about that. Tomorrow, maybe."

That suggestion was, among other things, somewhat premature. I didn't know if Abby could spare me two days in a row. Her recovery was going well, and Pepper was always happy to be of service, but that didn't mean I should forget the reason I was in town in the first place.

"Tomorrow would be wonderful," Winter agreed. My heart rate increased, and I was gearing up to propose a specific plan when she interrupted with a blast of disheartening reality. "But I have to pack for my business trip."

"Must be quite a trip if it takes all day to pack."

"I also have to prep for the job I'll be doing. Normally, I would have done that today, but I had something better to do."

It was good to know I was more interesting than her homework. "If you need help, I happen to be invaluable in the kitchen."

"That's not the word I would use."

"Really? What would you call my assistance?"

We reached her front door before she answered (though I suspect she would have chosen something like "beguiling"). I'd spent half a day with her but still didn't want to say goodbye, so I lingered on her porch. She lingered too, making no move to open the door. It was like both of us knew that me crossing the threshold would be a step too far, but neither of us cared for the alternative.

"Can I ask where you're headed?" I set the picnic basket and blanket down and held both her hands in mine. I couldn't seem to look away from her (not that I put forth much effort).

"You can ask, but I'm not sure I should answer."

"Now I have to know."

She scrunched her face into an apologetic grimace. "I'm going to New York."

"You could have lied. Told me you were going to an ex-girlfriend's house or a free-love commune, something less painful."

"I'll try to be more dishonest in the future. Do you want me to bring you anything? Some noise pollution, maybe?"

"I'd settle for a bit of culture. A museum would be nice."

"You're in luck. The Anneville Anvil Museum just extended its hours."

"It's kind of ironic that I'll be stuck pining in Anneville while you're off in New York."

"I'll probably do some pining too."

"But with a much better skyline." I leaned closer to her. "Thank you for today. It was the best day I've had in a very long time."

"Does that mean you actually had a good time in Anneville?"

"I had a good time with you," I clarified.

That must have been the right thing to say because she grabbed the front of my shirt, pulled me to her, and kissed me. As her soft lips parted and her tongue danced with mine, her hands moved down my body to my hips, drawing me even closer. Had I known before that night what kissing Winter would be like, I would have moved heaven and earth to make it happen sooner.

She ended the kiss as suddenly as she'd started it, but I moved in for more. "Good night, Avery." She touched a finger to my lips, as if that would stop me.

"This has to last me a whole week," I said and kissed her once more before finally, reluctantly letting her go inside.

The next morning Abby was waiting for me in the kitchen. She had a cup of coffee in front of her and a smug expression that I wasn't completely ready to confront. She looked more robust than she had in weeks, though that may have been the wishful thinking talking.

"You got home late last night," she said, all innocence, as if she wasn't about to pry every last detail out of me.

"Sorry, Mom. I will let it happen again."

"How was it?" she asked. "Give me all the dirt."

I poured a cup of coffee for me, topped off her mug, and settled in for the debriefing. I watched her reactions as I told her everything, from coffee to cooking to the best first kiss in the history of first kisses, and with each detail I shared, her expression grew more dreamy, like it was her love life I was talking about.

"That's a lot of fun for one day in Anneville. Do you think you'll recover?"

"You Annevillians are unduly proud of this little town."

"First, you're one of us." I almost spat out my coffee at her insult. "And second, when are you seeing her again?"

"Not for a week." I explained Winter's travel plans and our upcoming excursion to what had to be the world's tiniest Pride celebration. Really, I wasn't expecting much out of Anneville Pride, but I'd happily spend the day with Winter and the other three people who showed up.

"You should go with her," Abby suggested.

"On her business trip? I can't." Not that the same thought hadn't crossed my mind.

"Give me one reason."

"I'll give you two—you and Juno."

"We have Pepper and my increased mobility." She dismissed my concerns with a wave of her hand.

"Pepper isn't here twenty-four hours a day, and your doctor told you to go slow."

"Are you actually arguing to stay in Anneville over going to New York?"

I opened my mouth to dispute the claim but had nothing. She seemed shocked, and to be honest, the surprise was mutual. I loved the city, and under normal circumstances, I would have been itching to get back. But I had left under a rather infamous cloud that I wasn't ready to confront just yet.

"I don't know if I can show my face there. At least not yet." She raised her eyebrows in question, as if she didn't understand my hesitation perfectly well. She just wanted to make me say it. "Because of Meadowgate."

"Surely people have moved on by now," she said. "Haven't they?"

"I don't know." I shrugged. "I'm totally ostriching this. I just dread seeing 'hashtag Avery Scumner' splashed across social media. It's easier to avoid it."

"By hiding out in Anneville."

"Essentially," I agreed, feeling even more ridiculous than when the conversation started.

* * *

Of course, when Winter wanted Peter to butt in on her love life, he showed no interest in her affairs. No, instead of peppering her with probing and borderline inappropriate questions, he was diligently laboring over the Bedeviled Eggs Macy needed for the next shot in the Halloween layout they were working on. She appreciated his attention to detail, obviously—the spooky effect he'd created on the whites was exactly what the client was looking for. But she wanted to gush about Avery, and Peter was refusing to play along.

She'd opted not to share her joy with Gabe. Not that she didn't think he'd be happy for her, at least in theory. He'd been pushing for her to start dating essentially since her last relationship ended. But given his reservations about Winter's ready forgiveness of Avery, she doubted he'd supply the enthusiastic response she hoped for. Which was why she'd been looking forward to working with Peter—aside from his eye for detail, of course.

She sighed a bit louder than necessary and zhuzhed a plate of Pumpkin Cheesecake Bars, carefully placing enticing crumbs near the dessert. Eyeing her work from every angle, she made one or two adjustments before her frustration got the better of her.

"You're awfully quiet over there, Peter."

"I'm in the zone."

"Let me know when you leave the zone. I have some news to share. Dating news."

"Forget the zone," Macy urged. She crossed the studio and plopped onto a stool near Winter.

"Already forgotten." He set his work aside and gave her his full attention. "Please tell me this involves The Ski Shop Hottie."

"Her name is Avery, and yes, it does."

Peter clapped excitedly, Macy nodded her approval, and Winter needed no further encouragement to share the details of her date with Avery. By the time she recounted their prolonged good night, Peter had uttered a thousand favorable interjections.

"For the record, the city also has parks that you two lovebirds can make out in. In case you decide to move here."

"I'll add that to my pro-con list," she joked. In reality, she had no interest in moving to New York, and she worried what would happen when Avery finally returned home. How long could they sustain a long-distance relationship before it became more trouble than it was worth? If she was going to be with Avery, she wanted that to be more than phone calls and long weekends. Which meant she either needed to reconsider her living arrangements or, better yet, convince Avery to stay in Anneville.

She laughed at herself then, realizing how far ahead of herself she was getting. They'd had one date, and no matter how incredible it was, that didn't automatically equate to relocation for either of them. But just in case, she started revamping her Anneville sales pitch.

CHAPTER THIRTY-TWO

Winter picked me up on Saturday morning looking even better than I remembered. I didn't know how much of that was absence making the heart (or eyes, in this case) grow fonder and how much was thanks to shorts that had me wondering why I'd waited so long to admire her legs, an oversight I planned never to repeat. She also carried a plate of cookies that she presented to Abby with an adorably odd apology.

"These were supposed to be pie."

"Must have been quite a baking mishap if you turned pie into chocolate chip cookies," I teased and reached for a still-warm cookie only to have my hand swatted away.

"Well, you never told me what kind of pie Abby prefers, so I think the real mishap was asking for your help."

"She's got you there," Juno interjected around a mouthful of cookie. Cookie she wouldn't even be enjoying if not for my connection to hot, lesbian Martha Stewart.

"Not that I'm complaining, but why do I get apple-pie-replacement cookies?" Abby sampled her edible apology.

"Because I feel terrible about your injury." Winter shrugged, as if it was perfectly normal not only to take responsibility for an accident she hadn't caused but also to make amends through baking.

"For the record, you don't need to feel bad, but if this is how you apologize, go ahead and offend me any time."

"Me too." Juno paused her cookie inhalation long enough to chime in again.

"I suppose that's bound to happen if I have to rely on Avery for help."

"As much as I'd like to stay here and let you three gang up on me, we have a small-town Pride to get to."

My show of enthusiasm aside, I honestly didn't know what to expect when we left Abby's house. I'd been to Pride parades and festivals before, but those had always been in big cities like Chicago or New York. Even so, I hadn't participated in any Pride anything in the past decade or so. I'd been busy with work, and at some point, it had just seemed like more of a distraction from what mattered than anything else.

When we stepped outside, the obvious mood of the town was jubilant. Other people milled about on the sidewalk and in the street, like a flamboyant flash mob. Most of them greeted Winter as we passed hand in hand, and I marveled at how many of them had dressed for the occasion. The whole town seemed to be bathed in rainbows and queer-friendly slogans. Pastor Briggs sported a T-shirt with a cartoon Jesus saying, "Actually, I love the gays." And to his left I spotted my high school history teacher, Mr. Graham, looking more chipper than I'd ever seen him in the classroom. Regrettably, I doubted I'd recover from the sight of him in freedom rings and a shirt cheerfully proclaiming that he was "100% Bottom."

"When does the parade start?" As much as I was enjoying the people watching (trauma of learning Mr. Graham's sexual predilections notwithstanding), I was eager to get to the main event.

"This is the parade."

"What?" I looked around, checking for hidden floats or a spate of opportunistic politicians eager for votes and photo opportunities.

"We don't have a traditional parade. Instead, we head to the festival as a group, and our neighbors cheer us on."

I'd been so distracted by the overwhelming queerness of the crowd in the street that I'd completely missed the support along our route. The lawns on either side of the street were dotted with townspeople decked out in their suburban finery—they'd actually taken the time to make themselves presentable rather than dashing out in their housecoats to see what all the commotion was about. Children waved every iteration of Pride flag like sparklers on the Fourth of July, and more than one house blasted "gay" music from giant speakers.

As Sylvester and Cher battled for sonic supremacy, I couldn't help but be swept up in the joy and celebration of the moment. This was my hometown, the same town that had heaped guilt and shame on me for most of my youth. The same lawns that had held Bush/Cheney placards during my childhood now sported brightly colored signs guiding me to the Pride festival and encouraging my deviant lifestyle. The one thing I'd expected to find at Anneville's Pride celebration was vitriolic pushback from small-minded protesters (my parents most likely included), but that appeared to be the only thing missing.

The fest itself took the general good cheer and warmth of the parade and amplified it by about a bazillion. It spanned the length and breadth of Fletcher Park, giving residents (and a surprising number of visitors) room to mingle, eat, drink, dance, and shop at the wealth of queer and queer-friendly vendor booths lining the perimeter of the park. Much to my amazement, a drag show was taking place before a not unimpressive crowd at the far end of the park, and Mr. Graham (who had added a rainbow-colored feather boa to his already alarming attire) twirled inelegantly in the front row.

"Do you want a drink?" Winter thankfully diverted my attention from the cause of my future PTSD.

"More than you know."

Thankfully, The Anneville Tap had a small outpost near the swings. However, the line for drinks wrapped around the slide on the other end of the playground, and it wasn't moving. Winter, either out of an intense desire for alcohol or, more likely, the impulse to be of service, stepped out of line and marched to the rear of the booth with me in tow. We popped our heads in and immediately discovered the problem—the drink booth was currently a one-man operation, and that one man looked frazzled at best.

"Noah, where's all your help?" Winter asked.

"Gabe is emceeing the drag show, and everyone else—" He gestured with his empty hand while pouring a beer with the other.

Maybe I got swept up in the convivial spirit of the day, or possibly Winter's prolific volunteerism had rubbed off on me, but I didn't hesitate to offer our assistance. The drink menu was limited to beer, canned seltzer, and some premixed drinks. I felt confident that I could handle the basic act of filling cups and opening cans. That bit of kindness earned me a quick kiss from Winter and a fully obstructed view of Mr. Graham and his feather boa antics.

* * *

Winter didn't think she'd ever witnessed anything more attractive than Avery selflessly jumping in to help Noah at the festival. Winter stole glances at her as they worked, somewhat clumsily at first but quickly finding their rhythm. She couldn't help but admire the natural, easy rapport Avery shared with customers, resulting in overstuffed tip jars. When Noah informed them that he planned to donate those tips to the local LGBTQ youth group, Avery turned up the charm, netting even more contributions to the cause and in turn making herself even more irresistible. But then she went and eclipsed her own allure by promising to match the funds they raised. Winter wanted nothing more than to take her home and show her appreciation. At the very least, she deserved dinner.

Rather than enjoying a private moment of gratitude, they wrapped up their day at The Tap with Noah and Gabe. Winter's shoes were sticky, and she couldn't escape the smell of beer. Her shower called to her, but Noah insisted on repaying their kindness with dinner and drinks at the bar, which had a full staff and an expansive drink menu. Knowing Noah, he'd already told his husband they were coming, and if they didn't show, that would only lead to Gabe making a nuisance of himself. Better to get it over with.

As soon as they entered The Tap, Gabe called them to a booth in the back where he had an array of appetizers waiting for them. Wings, stuffed mushrooms, jalapeño poppers, and just about anything that could be breaded and fried crowded the table. Winter would have preferred something marginally healthy, but her growling stomach favored the immediacy of Gabe's nutritionally void offerings.

"I would have had drinks waiting, too, but not everyone's a piña colada lover like me." He batted his eyes and sipped from a ridiculously twisty straw.

"I'll take anything with alcohol in it." Avery sank into the open seat across from Gabe.

"Anything but beer," Winter clarified and collapsed beside her.

"I could not feel more proud than I do right now." He smiled broadly, and the glitter dotting his cheeks sparkled in the light. As soon as Noah arrived with a fresh round of drinks, Gabe raised his glass. "Drink up, ladies. Tonight, our heroes drink for free."

Winter took one swallow of her piña colada and wished she'd been more discerning, but Gabe's genuine pleasure in that moment—only twenty percent of which appeared to be rum based—came as a giant relief. Any reservations he'd had about Avery were seemingly of the past—Gabe, especially once alcohol entered his system, had never been known to keep his opinions to himself. The fact that he'd said nothing unflattering about Avery spoke volumes.

Winter sat quietly, nursing her drink and allowing the others to engage. She enjoyed watching Avery cast her charming spell over them. Within thirty minutes, she had them laughing, and Gabe began testing out pet names for her. This introduction couldn't have gone any better. Even so, Winter hoped for an abridged session, a hope that dimmed when another round of drinks appeared and Gabe launched into an amusing tale from his day at the fest. While she half listened to her friend, she gently massaged Avery's shoulder and neck. A soft, appreciative "mmm" took her attention immediately from Gabe's anecdote. She needed to be alone with Avery.

"I'm sorry to cut things short, but I have to get back to Abby and Juno." Avery held up her phone, suggesting that there was a message requesting her help.

A flutter of activity erupted at the table as they exchanged goodbyes and promised to do this again sometime—without the hours of labor beforehand. The warmth of the evening embraced them when they left the bar, and as they started walking, Winter took Avery's hand.

"Did Abby say she needs you right away?" She couldn't keep the disappointment out of her voice.

"Abby didn't say anything. I just wanted to spend some time alone with you."

"We should make that happen. Now."

CHAPTER THIRTY-THREE

The walk from the bar to Winter's house had never seemed longer. It felt like someone had extended the route just to toy with her. With each step, images of what it would mean to be alone with Avery flashed in her mind, yielding extremely visceral reactions in her chest and other areas to the south.

This had already been a practically perfect day. It felt almost greedy to want more, but she wasn't about to deny herself, not after all they'd been through to get to this point. All the delays, the miscommunications, the endless business trips, and every other hiccup along the path to this exact outcome made her treasure it all the more. She wanted to stop time and appreciate everything that had brought them together—a surreal thought if ever there was one. She'd used up more than one birthday wish trying to bring about this moment, and she wasn't about to rush through it to get to the good part. For her, all of it would be the good part.

When they finally arrived at her house, Winter stopped abruptly on the porch. What she wanted in that moment was for Avery to take her, to demonstrate just how mutual their attraction was. So, she paused before opening the door and turned to face Avery. Leaning against the closed door, she smiled what she hoped was her most alluring smile.

"Thank you for making sure I got home safely."

"Anneville's a dangerous place." Avery moved temptingly close. "I should probably check under your bed. Just to be safe."

"Are you inviting yourself in?" Her gaze lingered on Avery's lips, her imagination flooded with thoughts of where she wanted them to go.

"You tell me." She trailed a finger along Winter's cheek and jaw.

Winter nodded slowly and pulled her in for a soft kiss. Time slowed as they lingered there on her front porch, their lips and tongues exploring one another's, while the moon and stars offered a picture-perfect backdrop. Slowly, as the kiss deepened, a soft, sighing moan of pleasure escaped from Winter's throat. At that, Avery reached behind Winter to open the door, guiding them inside and breaking contact only once the door closed behind them.

"Can I get you a drink?" Winter asked breathlessly. She wasn't thirsty, but she needed a moment to collect herself.

She suddenly felt nervous, but good nervous. The kind that preceded something wonderful, like visiting Paris for the first time or the actualization of a childhood crush. She moved into the kitchen without waiting for Avery's reply.

She opened the cabinet where she kept her wineglasses but stopped when she felt Avery's warm breath on her neck. She grabbed Winter by the waist and placed several kisses on the delicate skin running from behind her ear to her shoulder, eliciting another moan. Her hands traveled slowly up to Winter's breasts. If her sharp intake of breath didn't announce her arousal, then surely her nipples did. She felt Avery smiling against her neck, and a jolt of pleasure shot straight through her.

She turned to face Avery, and as they kissed, she lifted Winter onto the counter and moved to stand between her legs. She slid her hands under Winter's shirt, teasing her stomach before dipping her fingers just below the top of her shorts. Winter pulled away from the kiss long enough to remove Avery's shirt and her own, savoring the look of pure desire in her eyes.

"Where's your bedroom?"

"Upstairs."

They stumbled their way to Winter's room, kissing and discarding clothing as they went, and tumbled onto the bed in a tangle of limbs. At the first brush of Avery's lips on her breast, Winter thought she might spontaneously combust. But then she pulled her nipple into her mouth, biting then sucking it, and Winter felt a pounding ache in her center.

"I need you to touch me." She guided Avery's hand where she needed it.

"You really do," she said, teasing her lightly before entering her.

Winter pressed herself against Avery, working her hips to meet every thrust. They moved together, intense sensations blossoming in Winter until she cried out. Avery stayed inside her until the last wave of her orgasm subsided.

* * *

"That was better than Christmas," Winter said once she caught her breath.

"High praise." I'd never gotten feedback like that before, and I honestly wasn't sure what to make of it.

"The highest." She propped herself up on one elbow and lightly traced my collarbone with her other hand. I shuddered as her fingers migrated downward toward my chest. "I've always loved Christmas, more than any other day of the year."

"What do you love about it?"

"What's not to love?" Obviously intent on driving me crazy, she traced lazy circles on my breasts.

"The crowds?"

"Not everyone is antisocial." She dipped her head to kiss me.

"What about fruitcake? That's vile."

"Is that a challenge? I bet I could make a fruitcake you'd love."

"Doubtful," I countered. "But I'd love to watch you try." Her mouth moved to my neck and started doing amazing things there. "What about all the expense?"

"What about making a budget?" She barely stopped kissing my neck, and I got the strong impression that I had no chance of winning this argument. Still, I was enjoying the effort.

"But dealing with family? That's awful."

"Depends on who you consider family."

She made a good point. "Fine, but even you must get tired of hearing Christmas music everywhere."

She shook her head. "Sometimes I listen to Christmas music in the middle of summer. I love it."

I was about to argue further, but then her mouth was on my breast, and I lost the ability to formulate words. She lingered there, moving from one breast to the other and back again. It was one of the most agonizingly exquisite experiences in my life. Meanwhile, her hands explored freely, moving everywhere, like she was committing my body to memory. I writhed beneath her, enjoying the sensations but longing for release. When she finally slipped her fingers between my legs, I was already on the verge of climax, but she teased and tarried, prolonging the experience and delaying my release until we were both sated.

"Definitely better than Christmas," I said. I was pretty sure I'd seen the North Star. When I opened my eyes, Winter's satisfied smile might have been the sexiest thing I'd ever seen.

We lay there for several minutes, my arm around her, her head on my shoulder, and one of her legs flung over mine. The room and the night were still and peaceful, the moonlight shone through her bedroom window, bathing us in its soft light. It was an almost perfect moment. Except for one thing.

"You love all of the Christmas songs? Even 'Little Drummer Boy'?"

"What's wrong with 'Little Drummer Boy'?"

"Everything. He's obviously a horrible human being and a lousy drummer. I mean, really, no infant, not even a holy one, would be soothed by drums, especially when played by an incompetent child who needs the ox and lamb to keep time for him."

"You've spent a lot of time thinking about this."

"Music is my passion."

"Even Christmas music?"

"Of course Christmas music. The first song I ever wrote was a Christmas song." I shrugged as if writing a holiday favorite was nothing special.

She sat bolt upright, her excitement palpable. "This is incredible. Which one did you write? Is it famous? Have I heard it?"

"Probably. It's called 'Christmissing You.'"

"I love that song." She snuggled against me and planted a kiss on my cheek. "Just when I thought you couldn't get any more perfect. How did I not know this?"

"It's not something you just blurt out."

"It is when your girlfriend loves Christmas." She looked startled by her own words.

"I didn't realize that was a rule."

"It is. Though it's kind of a pointless one now. Did you catch the part where I called myself your girlfriend?"

"You're not trying to take it back, are you? Because I have a rule against that."

CHAPTER THIRTY-FOUR

Two weeks later, Winter still couldn't believe she'd actually slept with Avery. Awkward Freshman Winter would be in awe. In all honesty, Adult Winter was too, not only because of some seriously amazing sex, but also because it had made Avery somehow more human and accessible to her, less the idolized fantasy she'd cultivated as a teen. She would have loved to repeat the experience. As many times as possible in any available location. She honestly would have taken up residence in her bedroom with Avery just to fully come to terms with the fact that they were doing the things that she'd only dreamed of.

Much to her libido's dismay, Winter had to work. Summer marked the start of her truly busy season when everyone from local restaurants to multimillion-dollar corporations geared up for the holidays. Normally for Winter, this time of year was second only to the true holidays themselves. She one hundred percent loved immersing herself in a delightful preview of the most wonderful time of the year. This year, however, she just wanted to be back in Anneville, spending time with Avery and learning all her secrets, naughty and otherwise.

As misfortune would have it, even when she was in town, her schedule overflowed with responsibilities that prevented her from devoting all her time to Avery. Had she known she'd have another, much more compelling option, she probably wouldn't have volunteered away quite so much of her time. But after years of tending to Anneville's needs and giving back to her community, she couldn't simply stop showing up. Not only would she be racked with guilt, but she'd also likely be sought out by well-meaning townsfolk and committee members who'd never known her not to show when she was expected.

Not that Avery wasn't also busy with Abby and Juno, and Winter would never want to take her away from them, especially when they needed so much help. But the tiny selfish part of her wanted to monopolize every second of Avery's time. They did their best navigating all the obstacles on their path. Phone calls—some of which made Winter blush—were a staple of their time apart. To say that Avery occupied the majority of her thoughts would be a definite understatement. Gabe noticed her preoccupation almost from the outset of the monthly Special Events and Beautification Committees meeting.

"You're smiling too much," he whispered in the middle of Trudy Vermilion's semiannual plea for more foliage on medians throughout town.

"I'm a happy person."

"No one is that happy hearing about herbaceous perennials. That's a 'Thinking About Avery' smile."

"How can I not?" She admitted her understandable distraction.

"I wouldn't hold it against you if you were sexting right now."

"I'm not."

"That blush says otherwise."

"I'm not sexting," she hissed, then sank lower in her chair when the mayor pointedly cleared his throat. "I'm ignoring you for the rest of the night," she whispered.

He dismissed her declaration with a fluttering wave of his hand and a text message that simply said, *Even if you aren't doing it, I know you're thinking about it.*

As usual, he wasn't entirely wrong. No, Winter wasn't considering engaging in any sort of illicit text messaging with Avery, but that didn't mean she wasn't thinking about doing other things with her, a circumstance that led to more smiling and blushing for Gabe to needle her about. The positive takeaway, she realized, was that if he was joking with her about Avery, that meant that he'd truly stopped judging her and started accepting her.

And since Avery was at the forefront of her mind when Neville Owens, locally ambitious *Anneville Bulletin* reporter, made his scoop-seeking rounds after the special events committee meeting, Winter couldn't help but gush about the successful fundraising for the youth center, particularly her girlfriend's vital role in getting them so far across their fundraising goal. Normally, she steered Neville toward the other members of the committee, who were far more likely to have and share print-worthy stories—the factual basis of which was questionable at best. That day, however, she decided that Avery's generosity deserved the publicity far more than the latest gossip about the peccadilloes of her fellow citizens. On a promise to provide the cake for his parents' anniversary later that month, she secured a pledge from Neville not only to run the story, but also to let her know when.

She wished him luck in his further pursuit of filler for the *Bulletin* before heading outside, where Gabe waited for her.

"Noah is testing some new concoctions for the Festival of Anns, and I generously volunteered us to be his beta drinkers. We can plan our costumes while he mixes up some Ann Sherid-anns or Old Fash-anns."

"Tempting as that sounds, I thought I'd give Avery a call."

"Maybe see if she's up for some in-person sexting?" He punctuated his comment with an exaggerated wink then sent her on her way.

* * *

Unlike me, Winter had places to be other than Anneville, so instead of devoting ourselves to exploring the physical aspect of our relationship, we were back to a largely phone-based connection when she was out of town, which happened a lot. We still managed to make what time we did have together count, but I couldn't help feeling a little frustrated that I was stuck in our tiny town while the best part of life in Anneville was off having adventures all over the country.

Not that I didn't have responsibilities of my own. Abby continued to improve. She'd even returned to work, on a part-time, work-from-home basis. Somehow, staring at a computer and making phone calls for a few hours a day left her exhausted, meaning our little family unit still largely depended on me for things like meals and shopping. I'd more or less fumbled my way into competence (or at least a few steps removed from ineptitude). With Juno's help, I managed to keep the house clean-ish and the cabinets full. I was on the cusp of cockiness when back-to-school shopping reminded me just how little I knew about parenting.

Abby assured me that Juno would be fine ordering her supplies online, but the one fond memory I had of my parents was our annual school shopping adventure. For Mimi and Arlo Sumner, education was paramount (at least the idea of it). They started every school year fully invested in my education, but generally by Thanksgiving, their interest waned. In all fairness, the feeling was mutual—with them focused on whatever it was that caught their attention, I had freedom to explore my own interests. Our relationship worked best when fueled by indifference.

But for that one week leading up to the first day of school, we all managed to get along and actually have fun together. Not so much fun that I could ever get them to buy me a miniskirt (or anything even remotely fashionable). Style disagreements aside, I remembered truly enjoying school shopping and thought Juno might too. That was my first mistake. She complained for the duration of the two-hour drive to a town with stores worth shopping in. Why was I dragging her all over the state for stuff she could buy online? She could be hanging out with her friends instead of driving past a thousand cornfields. Shouldn't I be a better driver by my age, and so on.

Once we finally got out of the car (without killing each other), she quickly caught on to the benefits of brick-and-mortar shopping, especially when it was my credit card getting the workout. Impulse buying became her new obsession, and I was too busy trying to recapture the bright spots of my youth to tell her no. By the time we got back in the car for a hopefully less contentious drive home, she'd bilked me for a complete wardrobe upgrade and a new laptop. (For the record, I hadn't really believed her claim that it was a requirement, but I also hadn't doubted her as much as I should have.)

I spent half of the drive wondering whether Abby would be more amused or angry about her con artist daughter and the other half calculating how many minutes remained until Winter returned from her trip to Salt Lake City (the answer was always too many). Then again, by the time Juno and I managed to haul the entirety of her back-to-school booty into the house, Winter would already be home, unpacked, and gearing up for the next excursion.

Overloaded with bags and packages as I was, I barely made it through the front door, and when I saw my parents sitting on Abby's couch, waiting for me, I shook my head, hoping to clear my vision. Had I inadvertently conjured up the specter of my parents by entertaining charitable thoughts of them?

"Hello, Avery." My mother's authoritarian voice rang in my ears, dashing all my hope that they were a vivid hallucination.

Damn.

CHAPTER THIRTY-FIVE

I hadn't seen my parents in close to twenty years, but they hadn't changed much in all that time. My father still waged war with the hair loss that had started during my teen years, though the front line in that battle had steadily thinned and retreated. His short-sleeved dress shirt (buttoned all the way up) hugged his middle a little tighter, and his facial hair showed a healthy amount of gray. His expression, however, remained pure disappointment.

My mother's face was less pinched than I remembered (more likely due to my teenage brain accentuating the negative than to any change of heart on her part). Her perfectly coiffed hair showed zero gray, suggesting she'd either sold her soul to whichever deity oversaw the fountain of youth, or (more likely) had become a bottle brunette. As usual, she dressed as if she was headed to some kind of high-fashion church. Prim and proper but never frumpy or outmoded.

"What are you doing here?" My mother's eyes flashed at the question, and though the last thing I wanted was to spark a conversation of any length, I followed up with something hopefully more palatable. "When did you get here?"

Abby's pained expression suggested that she'd been sitting with King Stuffy and Lady Grouch far too long. But since it was my parents, five minutes in their presence could reduce even the happiest person to pure misery.

"We were wondering the same thing about you," my mother said. Beside her, my father nodded solemnly, as if he was a judge instead of a henpecked husband.

The independent adult who'd been taking care of herself for decades no thanks to them part of me wanted to offer the sarcastic response they deserved. Fortunately, the much more sensible side of me that wanted to avoid an argument or any reason to prolong this encounter came to the rescue.

"It's been a few months."

"And we're only hearing about it now." My mother's well-worn frown lines deepened in her extreme disappointment.

"How did you hear about it?"

"We shouldn't know when our daughter is in town?" My father's booming voice filled the suddenly claustrophobic space.

Juno had the good sense to slip out of the room with as many of her packages as she could carry, but Abby stayed put. Just like when we were kids, she was there, shoring me up in the face of my parents' malignity.

"I was hoping you wouldn't." My mother's jaw dropped at my frank statement. "Don't act shocked, Mother. We haven't spoken in over a decade. You have to know there's a reason for that."

"Haven't you moved past that little disagreement? It was so long ago."

"Which of our many disagreements are you referring to? The one where you forbade me from seeing Aunt Aggie? Or maybe that time when you rejected your only child because she's queer?"

My mother winced. "That word is so distasteful."

"Sounds like you haven't moved past it either." I suppressed the almost overwhelming urge to start chanting "queer" just to see her squirm.

"That's not fair," Dad chimed in. "Not liking a word doesn't mean that we don't love you. We simply prefer not to discuss certain decisions you've made."

"And you don't see anything wrong with that?" I didn't bother correcting his belief that I'd chosen to be gay. It wasn't like he'd be any more likely to believe me now than when I was a teenager. "Do you honestly think that good parents just ignore the parts of their kids that they don't like? That loving, caring people would ever ask their children to stop being their authentic selves just to maintain an outwardly happy relationship?"

Neither of them answered, but at least they had the decency to look away in what I chose to interpret as shame. Wishful thinking, I knew, but that was as close to an admission of wrongdoing as I was likely to get.

"We didn't come here to argue," my mother said. "But we should have known you'd turn this into a fight. You've always been contentious. You didn't get that from us."

"I'll be sure to add that to the long list of things you never gave me." I went to the kitchen to get myself a drink. If I was going to deal with these people, I needed some kind of fortification. "If you didn't come to argue, why are you here?" I asked again when I returned to the living room.

"We wanted to see you," Dad said. "After we read that story about you in the *Bulletin*, we thought it might be time to reach out."

I hadn't thought about the *Anneville Bulletin* in decades, so I obviously hadn't read any stories about me or anyone else in town. Honestly, I was surprised to learn that it hadn't gone the way of most other small-town newspapers, but my surprise paled in comparison to my confusion in that moment. What story? Had they unearthed an article from my childhood? And why would that suddenly make them hungry for contact with me?

"Do you know what they're talking about?" I asked Abby, whose suddenly sheepish expression told me that she knew more than she was saying.

"I didn't think it was worth bringing to your attention," she confessed.

I had so many questions swirling around in my head, but before I could ask for some kind of explanation, the doorbell rang. I half expected to see a priest or some distant cousins there for an intervention (about what I still didn't know). Instead, I was pleasantly surprised to find Winter on the porch. She greeted me enthusiastically, and I could feel my parents' disapproval.

"Abby told me to come over as soon as I could. Is everything okay?"

"Not exactly," I said, stepping aside to let her in. "My parents are here."

"Oh. Well. That's, um, something."

I'd shared a few things about them with Winter but had spared her most of the unsavory details of life with the Sumners. Even so, her uncharacteristically neutral response to the news perfectly captured what all of us must have been feeling in that moment.

"It's a pleasure to meet you, Mr. and Mrs. Sumner."

Winter's typical graciousness resurfaced almost immediately, even in the face of my parents' hostility. They ignored her extended hand and scowled at her chipper disposition, at which point she inched closer to me and took my hand. If not for Winter's obvious discomfort, I would have enjoyed tormenting my parents with overt displays of queerness. Instead, I settled for the satisfaction of their distress at the sight of their beer-swilling, lady-loving disappointment of a daughter.

"Let's get back to that newspaper article," I said, looking to the terrible twosome on the couch for an explanation.

"Isn't it terrific? Neville did such a great job," Winter gushed, leaving me the only completely clueless person in the room.

"I could tell you if I knew what you all were talking about."

Without hesitating, Winter brought up the *Anneville Bulletin* app, the existence of which was as surprising as the article praising my generous donation to the youth center. While I didn't mind a little glowing press (especially in light of the influx of negative publicity I'd recently endured), that certainly wasn't why I'd made the donation, not that my reputation-obsessed parents would understand that. Even after reading the article, I still didn't know why they'd sought me out. If anything, I would have expected the news of my misguided (in their view) philanthropy to repel them. Yet, there they were.

"This still doesn't explain what you came here for. I'm guessing it wasn't to praise my generosity, so what did you hope to accomplish with this ambush?"

"We simply thought it was time that you let us back in your life," my mother said in an oblique attempt to shift the blame for our lengthy schism entirely on to my shoulders. "It could be mutually beneficial."

"I hope you didn't pull a muscle with such an inhibited display of affection." A long-overdue rant was on the verge of takeoff when the full meaning of her words hit me. "You want money, don't you?"

"We would never ask for money," Dad objected immediately.

"Of course not. You're too proud for that. But the only information you could have gotten from that article is that I have money to spare and that I'm still a great big homo."

My mother winced, and Dad sputtered for a moment without ever saying any actual words. True, I was just guessing at their sudden interest in my life, but their response did little to disabuse me of my conclusion.

"Either you came here to set me straight, so to speak, or you think my generosity extends to people who've only ever wanted me to be somebody I wasn't. But I'm happy with who I am. In fact, I'm so happy that I might make another donation to the youth group in your name."

I wouldn't actually give them credit for any kind of good deed, but my mother looked appropriately horrified at the idea.

"We're leaving." She marched to the door, never once looking at me. I'd never been happier to watch someone walk away from me.

* * *

"This is all my fault," Winter said as soon as Avery's parents left. "I'm so sorry."

"I can think of several explanations for my parents being horrible people, but you aren't one of them."

"I'm pretty sure they were atrocious at birth," Abby chimed in. "You are not to blame."

"Thank you for that, I guess, but the article is my fault. I was so proud of you, and I wanted the rest of the town to appreciate how wonderful you are. I didn't even think about your parents reading that story and showing up to try to make you feel guilty about being so generous." Winter said all of that in a rush, hoping that Avery would understand and not be angry with her.

"It's never wrong to not think about my parents," she joked. She pulled Winter into a tight embrace, adding to her relief.

"You're not mad?"

"I'm more touched that you're proud of me. I'm not used to that." She kissed her then, wiping away any doubts that Winter might have had.

"Quit being mushy, you two. Or go somewhere else and do that," Abby said. She tossed a throw pillow at them as added incentive to end their kissing before it progressed further.

"Do you really think they wanted money?" Winter asked. Even after seeing them in action, she still couldn't believe that Avery hadn't embellished her parents' appalling behavior.

"I wouldn't put it past them," Abby said. "They are notoriously evil."

"I'm almost tempted to pay them just to make them go away."

"Or you could trust that they got the message and stick with giving your money to people you care about," Winter suggested. "You made your feelings pretty clear."

"I did, didn't I?" Avery smiled proudly. "I might have to start doing that more often."

"Does this mean you don't want the framed copy of the article I made for you?" Winter asked.

"Are you kidding? That would be like the childhood trauma equivalent of mounting a deer head on my wall. I should get a laminated version for my wallet."

CHAPTER THIRTY-SIX

After the Sumners retreated to their lair, taking their dark cloud of harsh judgment with them, Winter noticed a shift in Avery. She seemed less reluctant to acknowledge Anneville's charms, even planning an outing or two herself. At her suggestion, they attended the Anneville Jubilee, the carnival that converted Fletcher Park into a wonderland of amusement each year, and she never once disparaged the event. No unfavorable comparisons to New York, no ungentle commentary on the simple pleasures of cotton candy and the Tilt-A-Whirl. She simply enjoyed her time there with Winter and Juno—for the fifteen minutes that she was willing to be seen with them before running off to join her friends.

Emboldened by Avery's decreased peevishness, Winter doubled down on the campaign to woo her back to town. For every disparaging comment about Anneville, Winter found two positives, showcasing all the community had to offer. In rebuttal to the complaint about the abundance of bland Midwestern fare, they sampled the diverse array of international cuisine available in town. They went to barbecues and block parties, met Gabe and Noah for drinks, and attended more movies in the park. They went miniature golfing with Juno, who had fun in spite of her mortification at being seen with old people. And Winter enjoyed simply watching the playful relationship between Avery and her goddaughter. It made their movie nights with Abby and Juno even more fun.

As Abby's recovery progressed, Avery grew more comfortable leaving her for extended periods of time, allowing them to spend entire nights together. On those occasions, they opted to stay in with the intention of watching movies, but they generally ended up missing what was on the screen, so preoccupied were they with one another. They actually started watching *Young Frankenstein* three different times but never made it past the forty-minute mark before abandoning the film in favor of time in Winter's bedroom—when they made it that far. On those occasions, Winter loved waking up in the morning to see an adorably sleepy Avery there in her bed. She devoted an immoderate amount of time admiring her and convincing herself that she wasn't dreaming. Avery Sumner lay there in the glorious flesh, dozing between Winter's colorful dragonfly-print sheets, possibly dreaming of her.

On one such morning, at Winter's least favorite part of the day when Avery was getting ready to leave and Winter was doing her best to delay that departure, Avery quirked her head and asked, "Did you hear that?"

"Did it sound like Abby telling you to spend the whole day with me? Because I definitely heard that." She moved in for another kiss and was just about to pull Avery's shirt off when a soft tapping caught her attention. "That's not Abby."

Shaking her head, Avery went to the door, where the sound was coming from. A moment later, she called Winter to her. She approached hesitantly, both curious and concerned about what Avery was pointing at. There on her front porch sat a tiny ball of black fluff. It looked up at them, blinked, and yawned before issuing a demanding meow, much more substantial than the little body it emerged from.

"Oh dear," Winter said and stepped outside.

She glanced around, expecting to find Gabe sneaking away or lurking behind a bush. She was certain he had something to do with this. Cats didn't just appear on doorsteps. Did they? Even if her friend hadn't taken pet matters into his own hands, there had obviously been a mistake. This kitten, who looked perfectly sweet and lovable, had chosen the wrong house to invade.

"Shoo." She flapped her hands at the creature, hoping to make it leave. Instead, it rubbed against her ankles and then stretched. "Shoo," she tried again, inciting further adorable antics from the endearing critter.

"What are you doing?" Avery joined them on the porch and picked the cat up.

"I'm trying to make it leave."

Avery's jaw dropped. "Who are you, and what have you done with the compassionate woman who used to live here?"

"Believe me, this is compassion. That kitten won't last a day in my care."

Any impact her protest might have had was repelled by the force field of cuteness created by Avery cooing and cuddling with the suddenly sleepy kitten. Really, how was she supposed to resist that level of adorability?

"How hard can it be to care for this little baby?" Avery touched her nose to the cat's, earning a gentle kitten caress on her cheek. Without even asking, she brought the precious interloper inside.

"I don't know. Ask all the pets I've never had. For good reason."

"You can't know it won't work if you've never tried it." Avery sat on the floor, becoming an enticing jungle gym for the kitten's amusement. They were making it impossible to say no.

"Are you going to help me take care of it?" Her reservations fading, she joined the pair on the floor, gasping in delight when the little beast climbed in her lap and curled up to sleep.

"I think you should name her Cloris."

"I haven't even said I'm keeping her. And how do we know it's a girl?"

"We don't, but that's better than calling her 'it.'" She reached over to pet Cloris, who issued a tiny, heart-melting purr.

"I don't have any cat tools. At least I don't think I do. I don't even know what to use for a cat."

"I'm sure Anneville has a cozy little pet store that can supply us with everything we need," Avery reassured her. "Let's go."

"What if something happens to her while we're gone?" Winter couldn't believe how quickly she'd moved from absolute disinterest to motherly concern. "We shouldn't leave her alone."

"She survived outside by herself, but if you're that concerned, I happen to know a financially motivated young lady who would make a good kitten sitter. Should I call her?"

"Yes, please," she answered without looking away from the softly snoring creature. "We'll wait right here until Juno arrives."

* * *

As I suspected, Carrie May at Anneville's Animals and More provided supplies, advice, and a referral to Dr. Jocelyn, veterinarian extraordinaire, who, among other things, could confirm whether Cloris was a she. Winter dropped an astounding amount of money in a relatively brief span of time, but every time Carrie May made a suggestion, Winter took it as cat care gospel. She piled toys, treats, food, litter boxes, cat grass, and a four-tier cat tower into her car. I couldn't tell if Carrie May was a master saleswoman who knew how to work a mark or small-town animal lover with nothing better to talk about than cats. Either way, she made a killing off us and may also have been on the verge of a kickback from Dr. Jocelyn.

When we returned to Winter's house (with enough supplies to start our own cat care superstore), we found Juno prostrate on the living room floor, completely still so as not to disturb the kitten sleeping at the base of her neck. The poor kid couldn't even lift her head to scroll through her phone, yet she seemed disappointed when I lured Cloris away with one of her new wand toys. Instead of collecting her pay and heading out to meet her friends, Juno stuck around, offering her opinion on cat tree placement and testing each of the new toys, rating all of them based on Cloris's level of engagement. I would have gotten a cat months ago had I known that was all it took to appease Juno.

"Shouldn't you be off with your friends rebelling against your sheltered upbringing?"

"We'll meet up after midnight for vandalism in the park."

She didn't even look me in the eye when delivering her sass. No, she was too busy cooing over the clumsy acrobatics of the newest resident. Winter was likewise preoccupied with achieving the best feather flicking to entice Cloris. I could have been on fire, and neither of them would have noticed unless Cloris scurried past me. Even then, they'd probably just marvel at how cute she was when she ran.

I couldn't believe it, but I was jealous of a kitten. I could have joined them, of course, but the floor was getting crowded with bodies and toys, and Cloris had zero discernment regarding what surfaces should and shouldn't be used as launching pads. It seemed safer to stick to the sidelines, at least until Juno left, giving me time alone with my girlfriend. Until then, I entertained myself with my phone.

I hadn't been looking for anything in particular, but when Meadow Lane's name popped up, I couldn't help reading the brief story about her rift with the producer she'd replaced me with. I saw Malcolm's handiwork all over the story, and I was relieved not to be on the front lines of the latest media skirmish. An added bonus, the unsavory story about me seemed to have been forgotten, as evidenced by several favorable comments and a lack of spiteful hashtags. That didn't necessarily translate to a career resurrection, but there was hope.

CHAPTER THIRTY-SEVEN

Cloris quickly took over the house and the lives of everyone in it, which, as Winter was beginning to understand, was standard cat behavior. She insisted on being a part of everything that really would have benefited from her exclusion. She scaled Winter's body to explore the counter while her harried human prepared food, and she climbed into drawers and cabinets that Winter swore she'd closed. At night, they had to lock her out of the bedroom or risk kitten claws in sensitive areas, but Cloris rejected that arrangement wholeheartedly, making her displeasure known with robust, mood-challenging yowls. Then, when Winter reached the nadir of her patience, the precious bringer of chaos would turn on the charm, rubbing against Winter's legs or sprawling across her lap for a lengthy slumber, and Winter's frustration melted away. Roller coaster of emotions aside, Winter adored the little demon and worried about leaving her for an extended period of time.

"What if she forgets me?"

"She's not a goldfish," Avery said as she lifted Winter's bags into the car. "Plus, you feed her, a fact she has never forgotten. But I can show her a picture of you every day if you want."

"Be sure to do it at mealtime." Winter smiled her thanks and fastened her seat belt. Avery had volunteered to drive her to the airport despite the obscenely early hour of her flight.

In a fun little departure from the miles of cranberries, pumpkins, and turkeys she'd been beautifying for weeks, Winter was headed to Atlanta for six days to work her magic on an Indian flatbread producer's national ad campaign. Since the company wanted both commercials and print ads, Winter had to coordinate with two different teams, putting Peter in charge of the still shots. Though she was nervously excited about such a sizeable endeavor, Avery reassured her.

"They're lucky to have you," she said as she maneuvered through the early-morning airport traffic. "You'll make naan-conformists out of everyone."

"Is it ever too early for dad jokes?"

"Not in my experience."

It was almost harder to say goodbye at the airport, where not only the temptation but the possibility for Avery to join her surrounded them. Had she left her back home, dozing softly while spooning Cloris, maybe she wouldn't have considered canceling or telling Peter to handle everything himself. On the other hand, canceling now that she was at the airport would mean that she woke up early for nothing.

"You should get going." Avery kissed her enough for at least two days. "I'll see you back here on Saturday."

The next six days were completely exhausting but in that satisfying, job-well-done way. Winter worked ten to twelve hours each day, setting up shots, making adjustments, and conferring with the art directors, photographers, and videographers to achieve the desired results. Peter handled the increased workload and responsibility like a champ, filling her with both pride and sadness. He'd likely be setting off on his own soon—he was far too talented to be her assistant forever.

His invaluable support and the seamless way he anticipated her needs would be hard to find elsewhere. And though she knew they'd remain friends, she would miss working with him.

"You look awfully glum for someone who can check off all the 'Life Is Good' boxes."

She jumped at the sound of his voice, not only because she'd been lost in thought.

"Aren't you supposed to be assembling chalupas for the photographer?"

"Already done. We've wrapped for the day, so I thought I'd see what you need."

"I'm going to miss you," she said and hugged him tightly.

"Am I going somewhere?"

"Probably. You're too good not to." She squeezed him tighter, and when she finally let go, she explained what she was talking about.

"I've actually been thinking about leaving you."

"I knew it."

"Do I have to? Because I don't want to."

She was certain she'd misheard him. "I would never make you leave, but you're so talented. It doesn't seem right for you to continue as my assistant."

"What if I'm your partner instead of your assistant?"

"Really? I love that idea." Not saying goodbye to the best assistant she'd ever had? She didn't even need to think about it.

"Then as your partner, I think we should bring Macy in as our official photographer. Make ourselves a package deal."

She hugged him again, thrilled with the idea of the three of them forming a company. They'd have to sit down and discuss the details, but that was a formality. She couldn't wait to get home and celebrate the good news with Avery.

"Let's do it."

* * *

As promised, I took care of Cloris during Winter's absence, even showing her pictures of her ravishing cat mom (which she did not have the proper appreciation for, in my opinion). With Abby's encouragement, I spent the night at Winter's house so that her tiny resident wouldn't be lonely all by herself. In all honesty, Abby was thriving and no longer needed much help, but she wasn't about to send me packing. And though I thought I'd be on the first plane back to the city once I regained my freedom, I found myself extending my stay. A major factor was Winter, obviously, but also, what was I going back to? Without work to occupy my days or a stunning girlfriend to spend my nights with, the city held less appeal.

Then again, without Winter to distract me, Anneville's limited charms also faded considerably. It wasn't all bad, of course. In my time back home, I'd come to know several of the residents and, impossibly, had grown interested in their concerns. When we met at the farmers' market, we would share the latest gossip, and I found myself engrossed by the lascivious tales of the seemingly upright citizens.

In the evenings, I often joined Miss Opal on her porch for iced tea and conversation, during which she regularly stressed Winter's contributions to the town, as if I didn't realize how often I lost my girlfriend to a meeting of the Street Sweeping Brigade or some other habitual joinery. I suspected she had a thinly veiled agenda, but I never probed for more details. It wasn't like Miss Opal was shy about expressing herself.

After the sun set and we said good night, I'd go back inside Winter's house and wait for her to call. Aside from missing me and Cloris, she seemed to be thriving in Atlanta. I listened intently to her work stories and plans for the future of her business, a future that might include less travel if her new partnership with Peter and Macy succeeded as she hoped it would.

On Friday night as I waited to hear from Winter, all the while watching Cloris scamper about the living room, I got an unexpected call from an indie punk band needing a producer the following week. They apologized for the short notice, but the guy they'd planned to work with had just entered rehab. While I didn't love being the second choice, I was ready to get back to work, and this could be the open door I'd been hoping for.

"I'll be there," I told them and immediately got to work.

When Winter called that night, I was distracted by a thousand tabs open on my laptop. She was so exhausted from her long week of work that she didn't seem to mind, so I told her I'd see her tomorrow, wished her good night, and went back to researching the band and booking a flight back home. On something more than a whim, I bought a ticket for Winter, too. I didn't know how she'd feel about hopping on a plane so soon after hopping off one, but I believed in my powers of persuasion.

I arrived at the airport early—I couldn't wait to see Winter and share the great news with her. At first, she was thrilled for me. But that didn't last long.

"When will you be back? I'll plan something special for your return."

"I thought you understood. I'm staying in New York."

"Forever?"

"It is my home."

"But I thought—" She swallowed hard. "What about us?"

"You can come with me, maybe get a head start on your new partnership."

"I can do that from Anneville."

"Well, then you can spend some time getting settled. My apartment is big enough for both of us and a cat. Or we can find something else. Whatever you want."

"I want to stay in Anneville. With you."

"I want to be with you too, but I can't turn down this opportunity. I have to go."

"But you don't have to stay. You can come back."

"Come back to what? My life is there." The second her jaw dropped, I realized how that must have sounded. "I didn't mean it like that. You know I want to be with you."

"I thought I did. Right now, it feels like the opposite is true."

I understood then that we were never going to agree on this, and my heart sank. "Won't you even consider coming with me?"

"No."

"Just like that? You didn't even think about it."

"I don't need to." The tears in her eyes suggested otherwise, but I was too crestfallen to continue pursuing rejection.

"I guess there's nothing more to talk about," I said around the lump in my throat, and continued driving in silence.

When we got to her place, I stayed long enough to gather the few items I'd left there, not that I really cared about a toothbrush or some tops (no matter how cozy they were). I lingered in the hope that she'd realize her mistake and stop me from leaving her house. Maybe tell me that she loved me and where we lived didn't matter as long as we were together. Instead, she watched silently from the sidelines as I packed up the remnants of my happiness and headed toward the door. In the end, only Cloris offered any kind of goodbye, her impertinent yowls filling the heavy silence between Winter and me.

I felt as if I'd closed the door not just to her home but also on any future happiness. I stood there on the porch long enough for the streetlights to come on and the neighbors to become curious, giving her one last chance to change her mind. She never even opened the door to watch me go.

CHAPTER THIRTY-EIGHT

For the first few weeks after Avery left, Winter relied on an overflowing schedule and a deeply ingrained sense of responsibility to keep herself afloat. But even as she carried on with her normal activities—as normal as they ever were for a woman who not infrequently created food-based artwork—everything she did was by rote. She shuffled through her life largely by muscle memory, leaving her mind to contemplate the split with Avery from every conceivable angle. And while she didn't completely crumble, she also didn't do much more than survive. More and more frequently, she retreated from social interactions, preferring to stay inside with her cat and her sadness. Even though Cloris was a reminder of the thing she was trying to recover from, she was also a comfort—at least when she felt so inclined.

When Halloween rolled around, she placed a bag of candy on her porch, disappointing the neighborhood kids who'd come to expect a spectacle from her. She'd make it up to them next year, assuming she pulled through by then. She ignored Miss

Opal's phone calls and knocks at the door. The old woman deserved more respect than that, but Winter just added her rudeness to the ever-growing list of offenses she'd atone for at some future date.

Not surprisingly, Gabe tried multiple strategies to save her from the post-Avery doldrums. Over the course of two weeks, his efforts escalated from texts to calls to flowers and finally a singing telegram performed by none other than himself, all to no avail. The breaking point came when Winter missed the Special Events and Beautification Committees meeting. Instead of bringing a modicum of reason to the proceedings, she hunkered down on her couch, her chest making the perfect cat bed.

Without knocking, Gabe stormed into the room, sending Cloris scuttling away to safety. He towered over her supine, robe-swaddled form and tsk-tsked. She sat up before he had the chance to drag her off the couch, but she made no effort beyond that.

"I sat through that entire meeting with no one to talk to. Do you have any idea how bored I was?"

"Sorry. I was busy."

"I can tell." He looked around at the mess of her living room. She hadn't had the will to clean, and it showed.

"Stop judging me." She pouted, hoping he'd leave her to her misery.

"Stop giving me reasons to. You're being pathetic."

"Hello, I'm genuinely hurting here."

"And whose fault is that, hmmm? You have no one to blame but yourself."

She couldn't believe he wasn't taking her side in this. What kind of best friend was he?

"Avery is the one who left."

"And she asked you to come with her, didn't she?" He folded his arms across his chest, essentially Gabe sign language for victory in a dispute.

"I can't live in New York. I tried that once, remember? I hated it."

"You hated it because you didn't have anyone. This time you would. You'd have Avery, who I seem to remember you being mildly obsessed with."

"*You* hated it when I lived in New York. And those meetings wouldn't get any more interesting."

"Of course I did. And I'll hate it again this time. But, as much as it pains me to admit this, not everything is about me." He sat beside her and took her hand. More tenderly than she thought possible, he said, "Just promise me you'll consider it."

She nodded her agreement, already doubting she could be brave enough to go.

* * *

I walked into the studio that first day of the recording session with The Vandal Vandals and immediately felt at home. Almost nothing exhilarated me like helping artists make great music (and I was actively avoiding thoughts of the one thing I found more thrilling). The band was as ready to go as I was, and we got right to work. I stuck around long after they left each night, mixing tracks and jotting down ideas to run past the band. Some nights I slept in the studio because it was easier than heading all the way back home to face my empty apartment. The band was easy to work with and happy to help me rebuild my reputation, but once the master was finalized, my time became far too free for my liking.

Unfortunately, being back home didn't feel nearly as great as I had believed it would. I tried to blame my sour mood on the gloomy weather because that was easier than thinking about Winter deciding not to be with me. Worse, she hadn't even wanted to try. It made no sense that she just said no and that was the end of it. In an instant, we went from incredible intimacy and a stronger connection than I'd ever felt with anyone to zero communication and living in different time zones. Facing a city of millions alone suddenly felt more bleak than bold. The one positive to come from my return was a decided uptick in demand for my services. Still, even time in the studio lost its appeal after a while.

On one particularly overcast and somber day in November as the calendar inched toward Thanksgiving, a call from Abby caught me between meetings. I answered immediately, hungry for a friendly voice.

"Juno wants to know if you're still coming for Christmas." She sounded aggrieved, possibly as the result of having a daughter in the throes of puberty but more likely because I'd missed our last two weekly check-ins. Either way, I hoped my answer would offer some relief.

"I already booked my flight. I'll be there on Christmas Eve as promised."

"She'd like you to send her the flight details."

"It's almost like she doesn't trust me."

"Well, you do have a history of disappearing." Her tone was gentle, but I knew from experience how quickly that could change.

"The active word being 'history.'"

"And you have been a bit absent lately."

"I've been trying to keep busy. It's easier that way." That wasn't exactly true. Nothing about this situation was easy, but maybe it would be someday.

"Still no word from Winter."

"Nope."

"I know she misses you."

"How can you tell? Because from here, it seems an awful lot like she doesn't."

"You could call her too, you know."

"And say what? Thanks for letting me know I wasn't worth the effort?"

"Or maybe that you miss her?"

"That won't change anything. She didn't even want to try."

"Sounds like something you should discuss when you're finished hiding behind your work."

"I'm not hiding behind anything," I said, not sure I was telling the truth. "And I still wouldn't know what to say to her if I called."

"How about this—you're being an ass and you're sorry."

"I'm an ass? How am I the ass?"

"You didn't have to move back. Airplanes exist for a reason. Just ask Winter. She uses them all the time for work."

"You honestly think I should live in Anneville?"

"I think it's not the worst idea. You could have two out of three things that you want in this life. And the city will always be there for you to visit. What's the problem?"

My mind searched for an answer, a sarcastic quip, anything to justify my attachment to New York, but any reason I had to stay there could be countered with an equal (or stronger) justification for leaving. I could make records anywhere (even in Anneville, if I chose), and the farther I was from the city, the less likely I was to run into Meadow and whatever producer she roped into helping her tank her career. In the end I wondered why I was fighting so hard to cling to my unhappiness.

"Good question," I said to myself as much as to Abby, wondering if I'd made a mistake and if Winter would even want me to try to fix it.

CHAPTER THIRTY-NINE

Against her better judgment, Winter let Gabe talk her into throwing her annual Christmas Eve party. What she wanted was to spend the holiday alone, reflecting on the past year and, most likely, reassessing some of her recent life choices. But Gabe insisted that self-reflection was what New Year's Eve was for. He claimed that Christmas without her party was no Christmas at all. It would be more devastating than missing *Rudolph the Red-Nosed Reindeer* or *How the Grinch Stole Christmas*.

"It's the social equivalent of a stocking full of coal. Children will cry into their pillows, wondering what they did wrong, and this will go down as the year that Winter Holliday ruined Christmas." He tossed his head, the ball of his festive Santa hat propelled backward by the force of his indignation.

"You could always host the party at The Tap," she suggested, knowing it wouldn't be the same as gathering in her cozy home. "Besides, I don't even have a tree."

"We can get you a tree." He tossed her coat at her and hurried her out the door. "I'll help you trim it. We'll drink eggnog margaritas and sing Christmas carols. I'll even let you monitor my tinsel-to-ornament ratios."

So caught up in the whirlwind that was Gabe on a mission, she had no time to protest the fairly revolting concept of an eggnog margarita, let alone voice her objections to this entire escapade. Christmas Eve was a week away, and having been in the throes of a lengthy emotional convalescence, she'd done nothing to prepare for a party. If she was going to do this right—and, really, there was no other way to do it—she'd have to recruit more help than Gabe, who could be counted on for encouragement and mixology but wasn't much of an asset in the kitchen.

But she had to admit that the thought of going ahead with the party had her feeling more cheerful than she had in weeks. She'd never skipped a Christmas celebration, not even the year her mother died. If she could find the holiday spirit then, she could do it now, too.

As Gabe drove to the tree lot, she sent Peter a text, asking for his help. She didn't know if he had plans for the holiday or if he'd be available on such short notice, but if this was going to work, she needed reinforcements, and she needed the best. Before they even parked, she got his reply.

I can finally check "Small-town Christmas" off my bucket list! I'll bring Macy too. Save us some hot chocolate.

She smiled for what felt like the first time in a year and joined Gabe as he scrutinized the blue spruces in the tree lot. As usual, he gravitated toward the priciest options available. Not that she objected to the cost, but she questioned the size of the tree he'd zeroed in on—her living room couldn't accommodate both that specimen of holiday grandeur and guests. Shaking her head, she began the slow process of luring him back to more realistic options. She assumed they'd meet somewhere in between Reasonably Sized and Inelegantly Ostentatious. No matter what happened, she was grateful for the love and support of her friends.

That feeling only increased over the next few days. She and Peter worked tirelessly to create an impressive menu of festive treats, transforming her kitchen into a veritable assembly line of cookies, pies, hors d'oeuvres, and canapés, all of them holiday themed. Meanwhile, Gabe and Macy fought with Cloris over the tree—which she endeavored to climb whenever they turned their backs—and every other enticing decoration she saw. The planning and work Winter usually devoted the entire month to came together in just a few days. Even better, she had fun with her friends, laughing and singing along to Christmas music. Of course, now that she knew who the creative force responsible for "Christmissing You" was, she lost the holiday spirit whenever it played, but most of the time, she almost felt like her life hadn't fallen apart.

The night of the party, as they put the final touches on the food and the tree—a never-ending task thanks to a certain curious cat—Winter realized that in all of their preparations, they'd forgotten the cranberries. She considered skipping them—they weren't the most popular item on the table—but it would be a shame not to have a perfect gathering. If she hurried, she could make it to the grocery store before Mr. Whitlock closed up.

"I'll be right back," she called to her confused friends as she dashed out the door and into the snowy night.

She made it to the store with five minutes to spare, waved hello to Mr. Whitlock, and raced through the store grabbing the items she needed. Arms full of supplies, she reached for the last bag of cranberries, but someone else grabbed it first. She looked up at the culprit and almost ran the other way.

"Avery. Why are you here? Don't they have grocery stores in New York?"

"None with produce this fresh." She smiled her disarming Avery smile, and Winter tried to find it grating rather than sexy. "Juno wanted cranberries, and you know how she can hold a grudge. What are you doing here?"

"Cranberries." She couldn't seem to form any other words.

"Here." She held the bag out to Winter. "I'll get the canned stuff. No one will expect much more than that from me."

"Juno should have them. I insist." Appalling though the idea of canned cranberry sauce was, she refused to be the source of any holiday disappointment for a kid. Or anyone.

"Can we talk?"

The way she asked, her eyes questioning and her voice full of uncertainty, almost made Winter forget being hurt. But the familiar knot in her stomach that mere thoughts of Avery produced of late sprang to life, reminding her of the dangers of letting her back in.

"I should really go. The store is closing, and I still need to finish up my shopping." She hurried away, determined to escape with her pride intact, but turned back at the last moment. "Merry Christmas, Avery. It was good to see you," she admitted before retreating down the nearest aisle.

All the way home, she regretted not telling Avery how sorry she was for giving up on them so easily. She almost turned back, but she knew the store had closed, just like her window of opportunity.

* * *

I stood there silently with a bag of cranberries and a thousand things I wished I had said before Winter ran away. Things like "I'm sorry" or "I hate the city without you" or "I love you. Please give us another chance." Instead, I let her get away again. Despite being the only two customers in the store, I didn't see her anywhere, and as she said, Mr. Whitlock wanted to close up. I couldn't keep him from his family on Christmas Eve.

Back at Abby's house, I dejectedly tossed the bag of groceries on the counter and plopped into a chair at the kitchen table. Juno sat across from me, doing some last-minute gift wrapping (which seemed extra pointless considering that we'd be undoing her work in just a couple of hours). Between us, a plate of cookies taunted me with their festive decorations.

"I think I screwed up," I said, and told them both what happened. "I didn't even tell her that it was good to see her too. And now she's gone and it's too late."

"She's not gone," Abby said.

"It's not like she vaporized," Juno added before slapping a premade bow on her gift for me. "She's probably at the holiday party she throws every year, which you would know if you hadn't skipped town."

I ignored the dig in favor of focusing on the useful information Juno had provided. Of course Winter would host a party on Christmas Eve, and knowing her, she welcomed all of Anneville into her home, which would undoubtedly be the picture of exorbitant holiday cheer.

"Why aren't you two at the party?" Even if she was mad at me, surely Winter wouldn't have excluded Abby and Juno.

"We want to spend time with you," Abby explained a bit too cheerfully.

"Plus, we didn't think you'd want to see evidence that your ex is happy without you."

Abby shot her daughter a look of extreme reproach.

"So, you were invited?" I asked, the seeds of a questionable plan taking root.

"The whole town is always invited," Abby answered in the most noncommittal way possible.

While that meant that, technically, I wasn't on the guest list, surely Winter wouldn't prohibit me from joining the festivities. And with her busy acting as the quintessential hostess, I'd have a chance to say what I should have said at Mr. Whitlock's store (or at any point in the previous three months). True, she might try to avoid me, but her hosting responsibilities would at least make it harder for her to run away from me.

"Want to help me crash a party?"

I expected Abby to chime in with all the ways that this was a bad idea, but she just grabbed her keys and said, "Let's go."

We strategized on the five-minute drive to Winter's house, and though our plan was haphazard at best, it was better than letting this opportunity pass me by. We decided (more out of nerves than anything resembling logic) that my luck would be better if we sent in a mole to assess the situation before I barged in on Winter's holiday. On the strength of that feeble reasoning, we elected Juno for reconnaissance and to lure Gabe outside.

The same line of thinking that led me to hide behind a child also insisted that I needed the support of Winter's best friend if I had any chance of success. (I ignored as best I could the very real possibility that Gabe would be more inclined to sabotage my efforts than to support them.)

As Juno forged ahead with an abundance of misguided confidence, Abby and I waited on the lawn, snow dusting our coats as the chill of the night seeped into our bodies. We watched through the front window, our view partially obstructed by a splendidly decorated tree and a herd of Annevillians milling about in their Christmas finery like attendees at an adult holiday prom. I spotted the reverend chatting with Mr. Graham (all decked out in a sequined dress that bore a vague resemblance to a Christmas tree) and averted my eyes before he could scar me further. That's when I saw Winter, more dazzling than ever in a green, mid-length dress that accentuated some of her best attributes. Her smile, though less radiant than the one she'd captivated me with from our first meeting, emanated such genuine good cheer that just the sight of her was enough to stave off the cold. She disappeared into the crowd too soon, clearing a visual path to the punch bowl where Juno worked to separate Gabe from the holiday cheer.

"Any idea what you're going to say?" Abby asked as Juno dragged Gabe toward the door.

"Not exactly," I admitted.

"Better think fast," she advised as the front door opened.

When they eventually emerged from the house, the sounds of holiday music and a dozen conversations trailing behind them, Gabe paused a moment before clapping his hands together and offering a puckish smile. That was not the reception I'd anticipated.

"The prodigal lover returns. What an unexpected bit of Christmas magic."

"You didn't know I was in town?" It didn't bode well that Winter had kept our encounter to herself.

"I'm not the town bouncer. I can't possibly keep track of every person passing through Anneville."

"I thought Winter might have mentioned running into me at the store."

"Wait, she knew you were here?"

"Yes."

"She knew you were here and said nothing about it?"

"Apparently."

"She saw you in the flesh and just carried on hosting a party like this wasn't a vital development that should be acted on. Vital information that she should at the very least share with her best friend."

His diatribe continued for longer than I thought justified, given the target of his irritation. As he paced the length of Winter's front porch, his voice rising with each lap completed, I realized I'd have to interrupt if I had any hope of getting him back on track.

"Shouldn't you be angry with me, not Winter?"

"Why? Because you made her happier than she's ever been and then deserted her, leaving behind a hollow shell, a pale imitation of my formerly effervescent best friend?"

"Something along those lines, yes."

"Of course I'm angry. But I also want her to be happy again."

"Good, because I need your help."

"If you're here for the reason that you should be here, then I'm at your service." He dusted snow off the shoulders of his red velvet sport coat and adjusted his tie. "What's your plan?"

"I thought I'd try talking to her."

"You couldn't have thought of that three months ago?"

"She's a slow learner." Juno came to my aid, earning twin glowers from her mother and me.

"How far are you willing to go? Because it's going to take more than a simple apology."

I suspected I'd be groveling as much for his sake as for Winter's, but she was worth it.

Gabe continued, "I'm not endangering my standing invitation to future holiday parties if you're not fully committed."

"I'll do whatever it takes," I promised, not without some trepidation. Who knew what Gabe would consider acceptable amends?

"Meet me at the back door in ten minutes."

"Okay. What should I do in the meantime?"

"Warm up your voice and be prepared for anything," he suggested somewhat ominously before disappearing through the front door.

"Warm up my voice? What the hell does that mean? Is he expecting me to sing?" I asked, though Abby and Juno were as much in the dark as I was. "How am I supposed to know what to sing?"

"He said to be prepared for anything," Juno offered unhelpfully.

"Why did I agree to this? What if it doesn't work?" I stood at Winter's back door, hoping I'd misinterpreted Gabe's enigmatic instructions.

"What if it does?" Abby and Juno said in unison.

I couldn't argue further because Gabe opened the door and pulled me inside, my pocket-sized entourage trailing behind us. A dense pack of partygoers milling about Winter's dining room eyed us curiously, but I had no time to react, intent as Gabe was on whisking me toward the living room where, I assumed, I'd have an audience with Winter. As he raced me toward a fate I was in no way prepared for, he made a quick phone call, alerting whoever was on the receiving end that it was "go time." Then he propelled me into the living room crowded with Annevillians, all of whom seemed as startled by my sudden entrance as I was.

I almost retreated (at least long enough for Gabe to give me some kind of guidance), but then I heard sleigh bells— in particular, the sleigh bells at the start of "All I Want for Christmas Is You"—and I knew exactly what he expected me to do. I locked eyes with a stunned Winter and started singing. Her subtle smile emboldened me, and as my confidence grew, so did her smile. We drifted closer to one another, and by the time I belted out the final notes, we stood mere inches apart.

"Why are you singing in my living room?" she asked once the song was over.

"Because I love you. And I miss you. You made Anneville feel like home again, and I never should have left."

"I never should have let you go." She took my hands in hers, and just from her touch, I felt feverish. "Not without me, anyway. Can you forgive me?"

"Only if you forgive me."

"I think I did that by the first chorus. I love you too much not to."

I didn't wait another second to kiss her, forgetting for a moment the cluster of neighbors crowded around us, drinking in every ounce of our reconciliation. Even after their collective "aww" of approval brought our kiss to a premature end, I couldn't let her go. Gradually, Gabe and company managed to clear the house of its human surplus, leaving Winter and me alone, still holding one another and savoring the entirety of this moment. Someone had dimmed the lights, and holiday music played softly in the background. When "This Christmas" started playing, Winter wrinkled her nose.

"Don't tell me there's actually something about Christmas that you don't like," I said, enjoying her adorable look of displeasure.

"I didn't say that I don't like it."

"No, but your face did."

"I just think that it tries to make Christmas sexy, and Christmas isn't supposed to be sexy."

"I wonder if I could change your mind about that." I kissed her neck and let my hands explore.

"Even if it takes you all night?" She took my hand and led the way to her bedroom.

"Even if it takes the rest of my life."

EPILOGUE

One Year Later

I watched from the corner of the kitchen I'd been banished to as Winter moved deftly between the refrigerator and the stove, her culinary expertise in full swing. Pots and pans covered all the burners, and every inch of the refrigerator was crammed with consumable cheer. The last-minute party preparations (of which there were many) kept her and Peter in a constant state of organized chaos that I found completely mesmerizing.

We'd been living like this for close to a month as the evidence of Winter's holiday to-do list filled every inch of our home. She exhausted herself stringing lights, battling Cloris's never-ending curiosity, and churning out a seemingly endless stream of Christmas delectables, all with zero help from me. Not that I wouldn't have happily spent all of my time with an enchantingly frantic Winter in the throes of holiday mania, but I was busy directing the Anneville Elementary School's holiday pageant and dodging Meadow's phone calls.

I suspected that the sudden resurgence of Meadow's attentiveness had more to do with the languid response to her flop of a holiday album than any real interest in me. As much as I thought I'd enjoy engaging in a hearty chorus of "I Told You So," I realized it would be even more satisfying to simply enjoy life without Meadow Lane. I no longer needed her talent to anchor my success, and I definitely didn't need her flair for the dramatic. So, I deleted her voice mails without listening to them, blocked her number, and put all my energy into shepherding the children of Anneville through a robust spectacle of holiday cheer. And while listening to twenty off-key six-year-olds scream-singing "Frosty the Snowman" more or less in unison was a truly singular experience, I was hoping to make this holiday even more unforgettable.

I'd cleared my schedule for the entire month of December, but once the production (rated four stars by the *Anneville Bulletin*) wrapped, I had nothing but free time, which I happily spent watching Winter work in the kitchen (a favorite pastime of mine). She occasionally asked for my assistance with minor tasks like opening the oven door when her hands were full or running to Mr. Whitlock's store for last-minute supplies, but mostly, I just enjoyed the view.

Outside, the snow that Winter had been hoping for started to fall (suggesting that even Mother Nature was on my side). Winter, however, was so focused on whipping egg whites for yet another magnificent party offering that she didn't notice the smattering of flakes dusting the ground. It seemed a shame to let her miss a picture-perfect Christmas Eve snowfall, and what were the odds I'd get another opportunity to coax Winter into taking a break if I didn't seize this one?

"I know you said no interruptions."

"I said no distractions, and you, my love, are the epitome of distraction."

I glowed at the compliment. "Am I more distracting than snow?"

"Snow?" She abandoned the egg whites and dashed to the window, wedging herself between the oversized pine and the wall for a better view of the scene. The childlike gleam in her eyes warmed my already toasty heart.

"We should enjoy the snow now that it's here," I said, though I doubted I'd get her away from the kitchen so easily. "We could go caroling. That's Christmassy."

"We're hosting a party in just a few hours, and I'm already behind thanks to someone." She blushed adorably at the allusion to my early-morning ambush. "Besides, only one of us can sing."

"I've heard you hit a few high notes."

Her blush deepened. "Those are *private* high notes."

"Then we can take a walk, just the two of us. I'd like to have time alone with you before the whole town shows up."

"I'm in the middle of making the cocoa hazelnut whipped cream for the bûche de Noël."

"Do you think anyone will notice if there's no bûche de Noël?" Winter and Peter both gasped at the suggestion that people would have a good time even without an obscure cake. "Can Peter make the whipped cream?"

"Peter has his hands full with the sweet potato croquettes," he chimed in.

"I'll pay you a thousand dollars."

"I accept Zelle or Venmo." He flashed a knowing wink at me, nudged Winter toward the door, and took control of the kitchen.

We walked arm in arm toward the center of town, our pace leisurely. Despite her concerns about what was going on at home, she didn't rush me, no matter how frequently I stopped to admire the snow-covered beauty of our little town or to wish neighbors a Merry Christmas. By the time we made it downtown (a little earlier than planned), she had almost relaxed enough to enjoy the excursion. On Main Street, I bought us hot chocolate with extra whipped cream, sent Abby a quick text, and then steered us toward Fletcher Park. As we followed the curved path toward the tree that I thought of as ours, Winter stopped.

"Do you hear singing?" she asked.

"Not everyone is opposed to caroling."

We rounded the corner by the jungle gym, and there in the middle of the park, surrounding an enormous Christmas tree, the kids from Anneville Elementary serenaded us with their enthusiastic rendition of "All I Want for Christmas Is You."

To their left, Abby, Juno, Gabe, Noah, and Macy waited until the end of the song (which, despite hours of practice, lacked any sort of cohesion). When they stepped aside, they revealed paper bag lanterns spelling out "Merry me?"

Winter looked from the message to me and back again. "I can't believe you did all this. When did you have time?"

"While you were busy making chestnut profiteroles and homemade candy canes." I tried not to focus on the fact that she hadn't answered my question yet. When I showed her the ring, her smile instantly put me at ease. "What do you say?"

"Of course it's yes."

I couldn't wait another second to kiss her. I never wanted to stop, but the world around us refused to stand still. Almost immediately, Peter texted, demanding an update. Our friends, shivering on the sidelines, requested a proper celebration somewhere warm, and our chorus needed to go to bed. I sent everyone to our house for champagne (and to put Peter out of his agony), but Winter and I stayed behind, holding each other close and enjoying the serenity of the moment.

She rested her head on my shoulder, her breath tickling my cheek. "This is the best Christmas ever."

"It's just the best one so far."

Bella Books, Inc.
Happy Endings Live Here
P.O. Box 10543
Tallahassee, FL 32302
Phone: (850) 576-2370
www.BellaBooks.com

More Titles from Bella Books

Hunter's Revenge – Gerri Hill
978-1-64247-447-3 | 276 pgs | paperback: $18.95 | eBook: $9.99
Tori Hunter is back! Don't miss this final chapter in the acclaimed Tori Hunter series.

Integrity – E. J. Noyes
978-1-64247-465-7 | 228 pgs | paperback: $19.95 | eBook: $9.99
It was supposed to be an ordinary workday...

The Order – TJ O'Shea
978-1-64247-378-0 | 396 pgs | paperback: $19.95 | eBook: $9.99
For two women the battle between new love and old loyalty may prove more dangerous than the war they're trying to survive.

Under the Stars with You – Jaime Clevenger
978-1-64247-439-8 | 302 pgs | paperback: $19.95 | eBook: $9.99
Sometimes believing in love is the first step. And sometimes it's all about trusting the stars.

The Missing Piece – Kat Jackson
978-1-64247-445-9 | 250 pgs | paperback: $18.95 | eBook: $9.99
Renee's world collides with possibility and the past, setting off a tidal wave of changes she could have never predicted.

An Acquired Taste – Cheri Ritz
978-1-64247-462-6 | 206 pgs | paperback: $17.95 | eBook: $9.99
Can Elle and Ashley stand the heat in the *Celebrity Cook Off* kitchen?